The Flaw in Perfection

BY

SMRITI

RIGI PUBLICATION

The Flaw in Perfection

By

SMRITI

Originally published in India

ISBN: 978-93-84314-70-5

Published by RIGI PUBLICATION

777, Street no.9, Krishna Nagar
Khanna-141401 (Punjab), India
Website: www.rigipublication.com
Email: info@rigipublication.com
Phone: +91-9357710014, +91-9465468291

To my Merlin & the Crescent in all of us.

If you are complicated and it would be Oversimplifying to say that you're obsessed with death,

If you are attracted to the darker side of life,

But also deeply spiritual,

If you are curious with the world and Probably quite intellectual and introverted,

If you like to study obscure topics and would prefer Your own world to the world around you,

You have GOTH soul.

A good many people, where Jasleen lived in Mumbai, came from single parent families. She's still not sure who her dad was and certainly her mom never told her. She always went by her name. So, Jasleen Kulkarni, it was. It was only her mom's family she ever met, so she reckoned that her dad was just a passing moment in her mom's life. But since her name 'Jasleen' sounds Punjabi, she assumed that he might be a Punjabi too.

What she remembers most of mom, was that when she was at school, she'd come and fetch her with this music stuck in her ears. You couldn't hold much of a conversation at home either because she liked her music loud. When she remembers talking to her, it's all shouting over Bhojpuri remix or International Top 40 at full volume.

She remembers the kitchen, with plates stacked up by the sink and she remembers wondering why there was so much washing up since they weren't a big family. No dad, no brothers, no sisters- just she and her mom. She supposed that most got eaten because mom often had guys around that she called her 'uncles'. Most of the time, these uncles weren't uncles at all. And then her mom would hustle her off to bed extra-early where she'd lie awake listening to Arjit Singh's Romance Hit-list until they moved to the bedroom and she could get some sleep.

Jasleen was more attached to her aunt in Lucknow, Sameera Trivedi, and she was only glad to have her for a best friend. Sameera would never miss a chance to visit her during holidays and help her with studies and assignments. To Jasleen, she was bold, beautiful, charismatic, smart and everything that she herself wanted to be.

Sameera's husband, Ketan Trivedi, was a man who believed in rules. Jasleen grew up listening to his Rules for Life on the phone. Some of what he told her were moral and probably the same things that most parents tell their children. She should never lie or cheat or steal or use the f-word, for instance.

But Sameera was far more likely to focus on the practical. "Jazz" she'd call her "never go out without an umbrella or at least a hat if you think it might rain." She would tell her. "Never touch the burner on an off chance that it might still be hot." She'd warn her that she must never count the money in her purse in public or buy jewelry from a man on the street no matter how good the deal might seem. On and on these 'Nevers' went. Similarly, she was told what she should do. Sameera expected honesty and integrity from her in all aspects of life, but she was also told to hold doors for children and the old, to shake hands with a firm grip, to remember people's names, to be willing and generous.

"Trust people" she would tell her "but verify. And love people until they give you a reason not to Jazz. And then never turn your back. Live without excuses and love without regrets." More than anyone, Sameera shaped Jasleen into whoever she was.

She remembered it all, as she looked at her star, now lying on a hospital bed, half conscious, after surviving a car accident. She held her hand and looked at her mom, who did the same on the opposite side. There was no other sound in the room except from a beeping monitor beside the bed. The doctor occasionally came in to check, and kept reassuring her uncle that there was no threat to Sameera's life.

It was getting late at night and against Jasleen's protests she was taken home by her mom. Not her home. Sameera's home. As they entered through the front door, they realized it was a mistake to stay there after all. Nothing much had changed in the house but Sameera's room, which was a complete mess. Tables littered with unwashed cups, a couple of sticky plates, books, diaries, clothes all lying on the floor…this was very unusual of meticulous Sameera. Surely something wasn't right.

Anyway, Jasleen was put to sleep on the couch and her mom went to clean up a bit with earplugs stuck in her ears. She rummaged through the junk around the bed in an attempt to make a little more space to move and all her sister's clothes had to go into the washing machine. All the while she kept wondering what could've really happened. Surely, Sameera didn't go crazy? She wiped the tables and shelves, put the books back, washed the dishes and swept the floor. By the time she was almost done, it was one in the morning, not that she wasn't used to staying up late. Picking a new bed sheet, she pulled off the dirty one from the bed when a sheet of paper fell out.

Bending down to pick up the paper, she was amazed to see that at a corner of the bed, there were several neatly folded papers with numbers written on them in sequence. And they were all unsealed letters addressed to Jasleen. She looked at the letter in her hand. It was number two. Where was the first one? Dropping the sheets, she settled on the bed and looked through the letters until she found the one. Before unfolding it, she decided to stack them all in sequence. There were about thirty five letters, all to Jasleen. The kid was just a 6 year old, what could she possibly find in them? The girl can hardly read properly.

Turning on the table lamp on Sameera's table, she sat down on her chair with a cup of coffee and made up her mind that she wouldn't get up before going through them all. Slowly, she unfolded the first letter.

Dear Jazz,

If you're reading this, it probably means that either I'm no more or I'll soon be no more. Physically, not spiritually though. You know I won't ever leave you, will I? And the reason I'm writing to you is just to explain that not everything in this world is black and white. One shouldn't define it that way, for there are a lotta things hiding within the grey. And, I think it's time you should be able to understand the shades of grey of my life, since my whole existence had been based on secrets and hidden facts. This is the story of my life.

12th Aug 2010, the day Meera and I joined Sreeram higher secondary school in 11th STD and I was remarkably convinced that I wouldn't last for more than a few months, surviving Bihari-Awadhi speaking-paan chewing-cigarette smoking-highly hot headed egomaniacs with no conditions or rules whatsoever. But, your granpapa was an army officer posted in that wrecked place, so there was no helping it.

Meera had no problems making friends though. She's always been better at socializing than me (I know, you that better than anyone) whereas I had problems getting comfy. Especially with girls, having gossiping as an all time job. And that means ALL of the girls. The only language I could speak properly without hesitation was English, that none of the teachers seemed to understand and eventually my classmates labeled me as **angreji maal**. Naturally I grew pretty attached to my English teacher, a

50 year old, classy, no-nonsense guy, as he was the only one I could easily converse with.

Dirty place, stupid people, weird language, spoilt students, girls often becoming pregnant (no kidding), suicidal nutcases, brand new trend of humiliation...took me more than an year to adjust to it all. UNLIKE MEERA. My sis and I had our own differences. She's talkative and ready to burst anytime whereas I was more of a kill-myself-in-silence type. She's more into painting as I was into writing. She would bunk class at any given chance and I would take down notes for her. Being twins meant nothing- we belonged to completely different worlds. A lotta people would tell me that I looked way better than her. But she was the one who had changed her mind over 18 boyfriends by the time we were in the middle of 12th std. Well, I was content with my guy Ketan Trivedi (yes yes..It's been that long) and my best friend Aryan Dubey who's been with me since. They were one of the 3 reasons Faizabad is unforgettable. Then came the second reason.

28th July 2011, the end of summer hols and my smile. I rejoined the school only to find out that my English teacher had left. He was transferred somewhere else and he left without a word. The only one who saw a spark in me, who encouraged me to be a writer, to be who I am. Jazz, how helpless I felt when he left. I didn't even know. He didn't even tell. And I lost a wonderful teacher forever.

So, for more than 5 months we didn't have a teacher for English at all. By that time, I'd somehow managed to make more friends with whom I'd play Truth or Dare during games and English periods.

"OK, not a suicide note" Meera thought as she went for the second letter.

Dear Jazz,

I know whatever I've said till now sounds a bit irrelevant and unnecessary. Hope I'm not getting you bored. But lemme go further.

December of 2011, something pretty funny happened during the English period while sitting around with my friends and playing another round of Truth or Dare. They asked me why I'd abruptly doze off during classes. I'd chosen Truth and outta a million questions they could've asked me, this was all they could think of?

Actually, I don't get sleepy or tired or whatever they were thinking. I simply close my eyes and listen. Listen to the noise in the classroom. I try to concentrate on that voice coming from the last bench which becomes almost impossible in all that mixed interference. I used to find it interesting, how I could listen to all of them simultaneously and make out each one but not distinctly. Of course, I didn't feel the need to explain to my friends about this habit of mine. Instead, I closed my eyes again.

"Aye ladki, do you see the future?" one of them asked.

"Yeah, I see your husband scratching the floor." I replied and they all burst out laughing.

As usual, I tried to make them out. Vidhi.. Sunaina.. Ketan.. Aryan.. Neetu.. Sneha.. Lubna.. Zainab.. Anamika.. Haider..

Suddenly, I heard everyone shuffle in their seats. I assumed that someone had entered the classroom. I didn't bother.

"goooooddaapphhhterrrnooon   sirrrr..." came   that   long customary chorus. I didn't get up, knowing that I was probably hidden behind the ones standing in front of me. Wishing people who don't wish back is against my rules you know. I didn't even open my eyes.

"Good afternoon everyone, please take your seats."

Whoa! I was stunned. Not because the stranger wished back, but because of his voice. It stirred something.

"I'm Vikram Srivastava, and I'll be teaching English now on..." he continued in his smooth...deep...Velvety voice...I had to open my eyes. I saw a tall, lean man, probably in his forties, wearing a green shirt and his hair neatly combed backwards. A sportsman, I could tell from his well-fitting black trousers. And probably...a dominatrix.

I saw Ketan sitting at the first bench, to whom the stranger asked "where do we have to start from?" I kept staring. He didn't look anything like that effect in his voice. I couldn't make out what Ketan said but suddenly it made the stranger smile and all the noise around me drowned. It was like watching TV in mute mode. I could feel the vibrations on my cheeks but could barely hear anything. All I heard was his voice, all I saw was his smile.

"Ok class, open your books, today we are going to..."

I closed my eyes again. I was floating.

"...a thing of beauty is joy forever..."

Truly.

Vikram Srivastava…yes Meera remembered the man. He was one of those rare people who went straight into her list of people she wanted to punch right on their faces. She didn't feel any different now either.

Dear Jazz,

They say, every dark cloud has a silver lining. A saying that for years, didn't make sense to me but was all of a sudden beginning to. I really was upset about my previous English teacher leaving but the new guy…wasn't so bad either. Not bad at all, in fact. It had been a long time since I heard anyone speak English the way it was supposed to be spoken. And this listening thing of mine started to become an involuntary action.

I remember how Aryan had once crept up behind me during the class. I remember him joking "try bhi mat maarna, maine suna hai ki vo pachaas saal ka hai". I remember giving him a how-about-I-bury-you-alive look and I remember being interrupted by a velvet voice.

"'Mr. Lamb did not die.' Who'll explain this?"

My hand shot up habitually but Meera sitting beside me got to answer.

I just stared at the man in front of me. Was I in the matrix? Whenever he spoke, I went blind. Jazz, I wasn't crazy. When I hear that voice, my world stops. And all that exists is his voice and my ears listening to him. There's nothing else. No noise, no other people, no thoughts, no worries, no yesterday, no tomorrow. The world just stops and it's a beautiful place to be in. There's only him. When he's gone, the world would start again and I wouldn't like it as much. I could live in it but I wouldn't like it. I'd just walk around, waiting to hear that voice again somewhere. Waiting… for the world to stop again.

I'd love it when it'd stop. It's one of the best things I'd ever felt. And that's why I used to let everyone think that I was just being lazy. Of course, Meera knew I wasn't. But I didn't wanna explain this to anyone, not even to that man with the mesmerizing voice.

"Crap." Meera muttered. How could somebody, already with a nice boyfriend, go crazy for a crappy old teacher? She returned after refilling her cup of coffee.

Dear Jazz,

It was a harsh-cold month of Jan when our 2nd pre- boards began. I'd scored pretty well in the 1st one. Got 93 in English. Not my best but cool. My teacher liked the way I wrote, something that made me wanna score better in the 2nd one. But, there was a part of me that wanted to know his reaction if I didn't...would he even care?

So, I nailed the writing section and screwed the literature. C'mon it was just a pre-board; it wouldn't matter at all if I played a bit. I ended up scoring 65 and though it didn't affect me so much, it was a bolt for my teacher.

"Sameera…" he said in surprise. I liked the way he said my name. "Explain this to me, Sameera." He pointed at my paper, looking straight into my face, unaware that I was melting into molten magma inside. It was very kind of him to talk to me about it in private, though he wasn't angry or anything as I had expected. I came in expecting a good row and there he was...giving me a counseling session. His patience and willingness to listen would always catch me off guard. I was accustomed to red-mouthed, hot-headed, **gawaars** who had problems in framing a single sentence without abusing. Not sweet-talking, mixed-fruit, sugar-sprinkled, muffins. My teachers had always told me to do better outta formality, but this guy seemed genuinely concerned. If he was pretending, it was certainly working.

The rest of the day was dream-like. I was constantly wasting my time thinking why would anyone on earth be worried about anybody like me? I had told him that my problem was time management and believe me it was just too awkward that we spent around 45 mins discussing how not to waste time. Honestly, I DO NOT know what he said at all. Whatever he said, went right above my head as my senses were too busy registering useless details. The sound of his voice, his intoxicating scent, the way he rolled his eyes, the way he wrote, the way his nose twitched, the way his thin, long, meticulous fingers worked...every little thing he did.

After that, I spent the rest of the day drowning in guilt. Okay, I didn't do up to his expectations but why was it bothering me so much? I knew it wasn't important. Anyway, I decided to apologize to my teacher like a good girl. And what happened? I ended up asking his phone number (I know, I know…) and did anything go awkward? No, he gave me his number without a slight hesitation and said that I could call him whenever I felt alone (dude, I was ALWAYS alone!)

That evening I lay on my bed thinking why the hell did I ask for his number at all. I didn't mean to. I dug out my phone outta my school bag (of course phone isn't allowed at school but who the hell cares?). I saved his number and simply texted him so that he knows mine. Nothing more.

Then came the real deal. Boards. And the 1st subject was English. My teacher and I would often text each other to discuss doubts. Luckily, there was no grammar section so that I literally killed my exam sheet gloriously in all my awesomeness.

Impatiently, Meera opened all the letters and restacked so that she could read it like a book.

Dear Jazz,

Days flew by and I finally got rid of my exams. Happy Independence day and I thought about hanging out with someone. Ketan was busy so I looked for Aryan's number in my contact list. As I scrolled down, I abruptly stopped at Merlin, the name I'd given my teacher. (Don't ask me why I chose such a name. I just did.) and thought if I should talk to him but then, I didn't have a reason. I wasn't like Meera, who could chatter endlessly with no sensible reason, no grammar rules, no social norms. So, I decided to wait for some occasion so that I'd have a reason to speak to him.

Days passed, nights passed, weeks passed, time passed and I was growing strangely impatient, until, one morning I woke up to his message:

Sameera, there's a msg 4 u on fb. Check out.

And there were fire crackers bursting all around my head. I wondered what was drawing me so much towards him as I opened my laptop. I found unread 2701 messages. Not a surprise, it had been more than an year since I used Facebook. I didn't check any one of them but went straight for Merlin aka Vikram Srivastava.

I found myself looking at a picture, which I recognized was a page from the back of my English notebook where I'd written a long poem for him (don't ask for the content). There was also a message:

Thnk u so much 4 dis sameera. I c in u the preface of an immortal epic... abt 2 n destined 2 dazzle the world.

I was dumbstruck. I couldn't believe it. He obviously would've thought I romanticized him or something.

tht's pretty unexpected..cant bliv u took it's pic..

gud memories r 2 b preserved.

....and that's how we began to chat every day. Initially, we began chatting in the morning or in the evening discussing science, physics, time travelling, laws, literature, people...all those things that people talk about when they have nothing to really talk about. Then we began talking in the morning and in the evening. It'd mostly include news, IPL, weather and books. Turned out we shared many common interests. A lot, actually. Then we began chatting late at night, often staying up till 3, on irrelevant anything and everything. Mostly jokes. It didn't seem much like a teacher-student relationship. We'd started sounding more like friends, discussing crushes and weird habits.

One day he asked if I wanted to have some fun. I spent a lotta time thinking about what kinda 'fun' could he be talking about. I was still in Faizabad whereas he went back home in Lucknow. Though there wasn't much distance, still a little too far for chilling out. I spent another minute on the word 'fun' before asking him what he was talking about. He simply sent a few pictures of his texts with someone else called Ritu. The 1st message was Merlin's.

Try 2 come out of moh-maya.

Not possible. 1st crush is 1st crush…

u'll hv 2 poison me

They r countless…hw cn I help each

I'm jealous…all r crazy abt u. ur eyes

hv sum kind of nasha…

tht intoxicates all ;)

Will v evr meet? Atleast like a frnd?

Wont b possible

Then tell tht u miss me.

Hv a gud day

1st tell me, will u miss me or not?

I'm hanuman-bhakt g

Acha…I'll b careful nxt tym ;): P

Ok, this was clearly supposed to be for 'fun' but honestly, I lost my mind.

Who is dis? (No comments)

A former student. She used 2 shout aloud her

feelings @ schl 4 hr eng teachr ;)

I…don't…like…dis… (I repeat I had lost my mind.)

Wht hppnd?!

Shout aloud?...hate it…

Ur language!

Is she beautiful? (I remember being complimented for good looks)

Didn't consider.

IS SHE BEAUTIFUL?! (Just a reminder, I had lost my mind.)

Wht's wrong??

Who is she?!

It's sameera…my wife.

Ur…wife? (I was blank)

Yes, sameera.

I passed out.

Dear Jazz,

The next morning, I woke up to Meera squealing "damn Sammy you're too hot!" what a disturbing thing to hear early in the morning… I was more used to just a "good morning, Sammy." But I couldn't help believing her words when soon a doctor from MH came in to check my temperature. There it was. 98.7 degrees.

"Did you eat something from outside, Sammy?" Dad began.

"No."

"Did you go out with friends to some wacko place, Sammy?"

"No."

"I saw you having those sweets that Apoorva aunty made. I always knew she wasn't a good woman." Mom chimed in, shaking her head dramatically.

I didn't say anything but I guess my grimace made my point clear.

"Are you depressed about anything, Sammy?" Dad continued.

"No."

"Did you...drink or anything Sammy?"

"No"

"Did you get scared of anything, Sammy?"

"No."

"Sam, you do know that you can talk to me about anything na..."

"I know."

He sighed. "You know, you were sleep talking last night."

I blinked. I couldn't remember doing anything that like. Did I blurt something? Even if I had, how would he know? As soon as the thought occurred, I shot a glance at Meera, trying not to appear too obvious. But she kept herself busy texting all the time.

The rest of the day I spent in my bed, convincing my friends on the phone especially Ketan that there was nothing much, since Meera had posted "my sis is sooo hot!" status on Facebook and tagged me to it. When I finally switched off my phone completely fed up, Aryan came dashing in my room. Though, no surprise there. I kind of expected him to show up and pretty much the same way he did. He stood in front of my bed, taking a good look at me with his hands on his hips.

"Aunty says you're sick."

"Mm-hm…"

"You pregnant?"

My jaw dropped. "What the hell do you think dipshit?!"

He chuckled. "You virgin? Guess so…or you would've told me.." he sat at the end of my bed resting his elbow on my feet. "So, what happened?"

"Nothing" I was tired of all the nagging.

"C'mon…somebody screwed your mind. I can see that stamped on you."

"Nothing really. It's no biggie..." IT WAS A BIGGIE. I HAD AN ENORMOUS IMPOSSIBLE CRUSH.

He began nagging again and I bailed with a "bathroom" excuse. When I returned, I saw him fiddling with my laptop. No surprise there either. I knew he'd dig it out anyway. I peeked in as he opened my chat with Merlin. I didn't care to stop him. He read the whole conversation, re-read, read again, gave me a shitty stare, then gave the chat another postmortem.

It took him almost 20 minutes to be done. When he finally looked up, I closed my eyes taking in the long string of bleeps that came next.

"Dude, why are you taking it so badly? I don't see how this can get anyone so sick!"

"I never said this made me sick."

"Chappal marunga, I know you ok!" he paused. "How much do you love Ketan?"

"A lot. You know that."

He gave me a hard look. "Know what, I'll just leave you alone. Think about your definition of love."

Alone in my room, I looked out of the window, thinking. I always thought that the best definition of love was 'an irresistible desire to be irresistibly desired'. And for the first time I wished I had never come across that definition at all. It made me so angry to even think about it. I irresistibly desired Ketan…but in my Merlin's case, I had an irresistible desire to be irresistibly desired. I wanted him all to myself for a moment the other night, which was a very unusual intension of mine because in my opinion no matter how much one may desire someone, nobody owns no one.

And this was just too BAD! I couldn't have feelings for my teacher! That too, someone so elder to me. It's just gross.

Dear Jazz,

Being a teen is not always rainbows and unicorns. It's the time when all the hormones in the body begin to go crazy at work. Life seems all simple and perfect until we develop a little more booby and booty and start feeling like a bomb. And my body was no exception. At least, that explained my loca behavior.

Merlin had mentioned about his wife before, but never her name. I never asked much either. He'd lost her in a terrible accident along with his unborn child and I didn't wanna press the subject anymore. I didn't wanna make him remember the details. Obviously, it'd have been a great trauma mentally and physically. So, I tried to hide my astonishment without appearing too cold. When I said that I could understand his pain he replied 'no one can understand me Sameera, beg to be different'. But believe me, I did. For some strange reason, I could.

Now, the problem at hand was that I couldn't get him outta my head. And I knew that it was extremely unhealthy to have inappropriate feelings for him. C'mon, he's my teacher! Who likes a teacher?! All those teen students deserve an award for standing their soul-numbing lectures and not setting their schools on fire with them in it!

And yet, here I was…losing to another teacher… I looked for my laptop.

Gud mrng sir

Gm cindrella

Can I say sumthng..

Sure anything

I'm sry... I lost my mind last night...

Sameera, ur name is d same as my wife's

..tht's all. It's ok.

Hmm…tht ws news 2 me...

Hmm...u both hv similr prsnalities too.

Really?..like??

Same fair complexion..long hair..tall..

She used 2 write too?

No, she ws bubbly. U r quiet nd patient

I hvnt startd yet... ;)

Hahaha…

Really. i can b crazy all d tym nowadays

Y so?

U shud kno…i'm under ur spell.

O… Tht's fatal…

It is nd u r d 1 2 blame! :D

Hey ram! Y?!

Temme wht did u do 2 me??

I've done nthng g!

Ok. Lemme make it clear in case you are wondering what the hell. Apparently, my body told my brain to F- off and everything that I was texting came from my primary memory, without getting processed, instead of secondary memory of my hard disk. Probably, he could sense that too. Maybe that's why he lemme ramble on for hours about how much he meant to me. I had absolutely no control over my words. I'd never felt this way before. Not when we were at school. Not when I could see him every day. Though, his voice lured me everywhere, he himself didn't seem to attract me the least. Yes, I'd notice the little things he did, but never in a romantic way. Yeah, I'd ask him stupid questions, but never to grab his attention but to hear him speak. I'd end up following him around the school, but it was never intentionally.

And now, I was falling. Hard. Like I'd never fallen before. I wasn't the first one to fall for his fancy. I wasn't the first crush-case he was handling. Yet, he didn't mind listening till I was finally outta words. I began to doubt if he was online at all. But he was. After a long uncomfortable pause he replied

Sameera it's jz a crush. It'll fade wid time.hppns @ ur age…I know wht u

r saying but these words r very common

2 my ears. Evn lord Krishna cannot

Return so mny crushes…

k. I get it. U don't hv 2 bliv me.

U deserve sum1 better sameera. U'll nvr kno hw amazing u r. u deserve sum1

Who's atleast not hauntd by d past…

a gr8 part of me is irretrievably lost

…lemme save d remaining

Everything's gone wid d wind …

Wind's nvr particular abt its direction

Idk hw 2 make u undrstnd...

Try. *smirk*

I'm way oldr sameera…I'm more than 50

..U r jz 17...

Hw dz tht matter... (Stupid yeah, I know. But I had to try.)

I'll b gone soon, leaving u all alone. Ur calligraphy isn't 4 painful poetry…

I get it…

U do?

Hmm..yeah

Gud girl ☺

So...

So?

Hw abt spending d rest of d tym wid me?

Jazz, what can I say…I was so nuts...and so unstoppable. He said he'd think about it and wished me good night before going offline. Of course, he'd think about it, wouldn't he? Being insomaniac, he had lotta time to think. IF he wants to…

Dear jazz,

I woke up with a start the next morning, all sweaty and dazed, to see someone with my own face towering above be, staring at my face. When I recognized Meera, I wished I hadn't opened my eyes at all.

"Morning Sammy."

I let out a moan in reply.

"What happened? You were crying in your sleep."

"Nothing…" I touched my damp face and looked at my equally damp pillow." I don't know…i don't remember." I blinked.

"Aein..?" she gave me a doubtful look.

I hopped outta my bed which itself had begun to gimme a sick feeling and headed for a shower, removing and throwing my clothes anywhere on my way. I stepped under the shower with my phone, carefully keeping it away from the water in one hand. I scrolled down my contacts for Merlin to text him good morning. I was ready for a 3rd rejection.

To my surprise, his reply was instant and rather contradictory.

Gm sameera, it's thoroughly flattering to be admired

By the most beautiful damsel of them all…

My eyes widened at 'thoroughly flattering'. Was he accepting me? Or was he trying to politely reject? I spent several minutes just analyzing it. Unsure what to say, I sent him a blushing emoticon.

And, like that we began to chat away again like we used to- flirty but friendly. In between, he blurted that his DOB was 1981. Dude, that means he's no way around 50! But I was careful not to let him know that I noticed. I wanted to see what more I could talk out of him.

Aryan and Ketan came by to see me, another surprise, with a teddy bear. Apparently, it was Aryan who wanted Ketan to gemme a teddy and I knew exactly why. He was worried that I was getting distracted from him and I can't say I wasn't. But, c'mon, I LOVE Ketan. We'd been together for more than an year and were totally inseparable. When we used to be at school all my jealous girlfriends would keep asking how we never had a single argument. It's because we loved each other, love each other and will always love each other.

Anyway, Ketan left within an hour leaving just the 3 of us in the room. Aryan and Meera looked at each other before looking at me in anticipation. The silence was too weird to stand and so were the deadly vibes I was getting from Meera.

"What? Why such faces?" I asked.

"I know what's going on ok? I checked all the messages on your phone. I knew something was wrong the very day I heard you sleep-talk." She said sternly.

I turned towards Aryan. He had his I-know-nothing mask on.

"Sammy listen," she continued and I knew an hour-long speech was on its way. "..I know that old guy is charming and charismatic and all and yeah…a bit hot but c'mon..." on she went..

I didn't try to interrupt her, nor did Aryan who was nodding absently to her every single word. We knew interrupting, objecting, pointing or anything would only make it worse. And what could I have said anyway? She was so right.

Dear jazz,

I must admit, I was stupidly, crazily and uselessly, head over heels in love with my Merlin. I was, quite obviously, more into men than boys my age but I had always kept that taste to myself. Then this man invaded my world and set me ablaze. He was such a sweet pain.

For months our friendship flourished and everyday I'd end up telling him that I love him. He'd say that I was causing him extreme distress by not treating myself right and then I'd be the guilty party. While texting him, I'd completely forget about anybody else online. In fact, he'd become the only reason I'd use Facebook at all. I had started spending my days writing poems, reading the kinda books I never gave much attention to and begun worshipping Nicholas Sparks over Robert Ludlum. He was such a bad ecstasy…my all time favorite drug. I was addicted forever.

But obviously and of course he didn't believe me. And his reason for not believing was reasonable too. By the age of 12 I was genuinely convinced that I would marry Shahid Kapur (don't laugh… I was a great fan). But that changed after I met Ketan. And now Ketan had become seemingly secondary because of Merlin. So there is a chance that may be one day… Whatever.

One day, late at night, we were texting again. We were talking about drugs and addictions, I was telling him how intoxicating his voice was to me and how I'd distract myself by listening to Ed Sheeran. They'd sound almost alike, except Merlin would take me high.

Hi, u up?

Yeah. U kno, I cn stay up late.

Wht r u doing, up so late?

Listening 2 ed sheeran…

Listening 2 me? ;) Wht r d lyrics?

Giv me luv lyk her...

Hmm…I know

Paint splattered tear drops on my shirt...

Yes...

Ok...so, he was relating the lyrics to himself...better. I decided to skip a few lines to see if it happens.

May b I'll call u 2nyt...

He went offline after a pause. I thought for a moment if I was busted and he knew I was playing. Suddenly, my phone began to sing Beyonce breaking my thought.

Merlin calling...

I chuckled, my heart pounding, as I picked up.

"Hello?"

"Hello Sameera," came a gentle but electrifying voice. "Then?"it took me a while to realize that he was asking for the lyrics.

"...when my blood is drowning in alcohol..." I sang out in glee.

"Haha...I know what happens when my blood drowns in alcohol."

"You drink?"

"Used to. Who doesn't? Especially after the incident?"

"Oh...how does it feel?"

"You don't know? High."

"What does 'high' feel like?"

"Good...in El Dorado and euphoria though."

"Maybe I should try once..."

"Mm...nothing wrong in trying. But in supervision.

"supervision?! I'll be grounded for eternity!"

He laughed. "Hmm…Ms. Kulkarni."

"I'll be in Lucknow next month. We can meet. Then, why don't you buy me a drink? I'll drink under your supervision." I flirted. Again.

"Well, are you 18?"

"Would you buy me a drink if I am?"

"Can we continue this later? I'm kinda busy here…lets speak some other time ok?"

"Hmm..."

"Good night Sameera, sleep well. Bye"

"Bye, good night..." I heard him hang up. "I miss you..." I whispered to no one. Good thing, he hung up. I didn't wanna sound like a despo anyway.

It felt so irritatingly great you know, this game of rejecting and still wanting. He had rejected me but deep down I knew he didn't want to. He had never said what he thought of me or if he felt the same way, yet he never stopped speaking to me. Always a mystery, always a puzzle, always keeping me guessing.

Dear Jazz,

I believe in Marilyn Monroe. I believe everything happens for a reason. I believe, people change so that you can learn to let go. I believe, things go wrong, so that you can appreciate them when they're right. You believe in lies so that you eventually learn to trust no one but yourself and sometimes good things fall apart so that better things can fall in together.

One of my darkest fears, Jazz, had come true, though I don't know see why. Maybe, being elder and wiser, my Merlin could see that I was emotionally cheating Ketan (yeah! I was stupid enough to tell him about my boyfriend at school! Go on curse me!) As well as my very self. Or maybe I wasn't good enough for him to continue with. After our conversation on the phone that night, he hadn't texted or spoken or anything at all for days. I remember he said that he was busy with work and I do believe it, but what I couldn't understand was, what was keeping him from texting when he could clearly read my messages. At least that's what my Facebook indicator was telling me.

It was frustrating the hell outta me and though I didn't make an exhibition of it, Meera could clearly sense it.

One evening, I was sitting on my bed, my chin resting on my knees, and my eyes staring at the screen of my phone, my body rocking back and forth in anticipation. No, desperation. Meera couldn't take it any longer. I remember how she stood towering above me, making me shift my eyes from my phone to her. She looked square at my face.

"We need to talk." She ordered.

I nodded.

"Not here. Let's go shopping."

I nodded.

"You don't have to take money, I've enough."

That meant no shopping, just looking. Anyway, I nodded.

"Change your clothes and leave your phone right here. We DO NOT need it.

I nodded, waiting for her to get outta the room. I was in no mood to go out but it was better than arguing with her.

We set out on foot to Awantika Restaurant with my mute phone safely tucked in the back pocket of jeans under a long kurti. She ordered a chocolate ice cream for me and nothing for herself, which meant that she was gonna be acting all big sissy to eat the next 30 minutes of my life. However she waited for the ice cream to come first, which also meant that whatever she was gonna tell me, it was something I wasn't gonna like.

"Sammy, I wanna tell you something. You listening?"

"Mm..." I responded, engrossed in my ice cream.

"About that Prince Jerk of yours."

"Don't say that…Ketan's diamond."

"Not him. I'm talking about that English-wala."

I sighed. I really, really didn't want this.

"Sam, you know I mean good. I'm your big sis right."

She's just 3mins elder to me, acting all 30 year old.

"I don't understand what's possessing you girl." She continued. "I'll come straight to the point. I know he stopped texting you for good, thankfully. You need to forget him ok? Ketan's great and so very understanding. It takes a lot for a boyfriend to know that his girl is crushing badly on someone else and still be willing to give her space."

I looked up at her questioningly. "Ketan knows?"

"Ketan knows. Knew it before anyone of us. Knew this would happen from the very beginning."

I got back to my ice cream. I knew he was smart.

"You poor little fool, you have to come out of your fantasy. I'm sure that English-wala has done this before. Plucked some good looking innocent student before you, and I'm sure he'll do it again. In fact, I think he is doing it already. That's what keeps him from talking to you."

I stopped in stunned silence for a moment, absorbing her harsh words. She looked at me with dancing eyes thinking she's funny. How could she be so cruel?

"Don't you learn things, Sammy?"

A lot! I wanted to shout. A lot of what she called the illusion of love. The best way is to share your body but never your heart. That's what her signature quote was.

"He liked me…" was all I could choke out.

"Of course he didn't like you. He doesn't like anyone. Not you, no his wife, not even his pathetic self."

"STOP IT!" I screamed out. The whole restaurant silenced. I saw a waiter approach us, but quickly walked away when shot him a glance. I turned back to Meera who looked indifferent and I instantly realized why she chose this place to talk. I tried to compose myself.

"Stop interfering in my stuff Meera, you don't have to tell me what to do. Just keep the hell out."

"I've been trying to help you."

"Well, you are not. You are just trying to turn me into a freak like you. You drive all your boyfriends away. You drove the very guy who loved you away and soon you'll drive me away too. No one can stand you for long!" I didn't realize how high my voice was going with each word. I was so angry, I couldn't express myself. She seemed surprised at my reaction. And that's a rare expression to see on her face.

Dear jazz,

Days turned into weeks and there still wasn't a word from Merlin. I didn't call him or anything. I just waited. I was way too proud to text him after a limit. Instead, I was all over Ketan. I grew overly possessive for him. We met more often, called more often, argued more often, made up more often. I'd call him home or go to his place, walk in parks, ride on his bike, go for movies, eat at restaurants, workout at gym together or simply just sit somewhere and talk. I wanted to see him more and more each day. Whenever we'd be together, I'd hold his hand or grab his arm or put my arm around his waist with his on my shoulder or sit on his lap surrounded by his embrace.

To speak the truth, Jazz, these were the things I wanted to do with Merlin. I missed him and wanted him like crazy. I'd be with him whenever I'd be with Ketan. I'd hear to find a hint of his voice in Ketan's voice. I'd look for his grey hair in Ketan's jet-black hair. I'd smell searching for his scent on Ketan's shirt. I had only been close to Merlin once at school and yet I knew the way he smelt. It was like a long lost memory clinging to me.

I was thinking about the same, as I walked back home from yet another date with Ketan, when suddenly a thought struck me. What if Meera had been right? Did I really mean absolutely nothing to my Merlin? I slung open the door of my house and went in as if dazed. Was I just another pretty girl he was trying to get rid of? Was I craving for something that'll never be? I was gasping as I entered my room imagining myself crashing head first into the old mosaic floor. I saw Meera turn her head from a book she was reading. The last thing I wanted was her to see the nakedness of my pain and humiliation. I could've done anything to prove her wrong, anything to prove that I was different from her. I wondered if that was why I was drowning myself in a hopeless love for my Merlin.

I turned on my heels to flee from the place. The corridor seemed to last forever and my body moved as if in slow motion, my heartache dragging me down like chains around my feet. Dashing, stumbling and struggling, I finally got to my neighbor's familiar front door that old woman held open for me.

"Namaste naani, is Aryan home?"

I'll never forget the pain of that heartache Jazz, it was as if I was physically sick. By the time I got to Aryan's room, I was hyperventilating, choked with emotions and unable to breathe. Images of my Merlin being with another woman flashed before me. And the woman looked so much like me. I was crouching in front of Aryan's door, where he stood in confusion and bewilderment. He had to almost drag me inside. I couldn't even reach a chair or his bed. I curled up on the floor in a foetal position, tearless but sobbing inside. Aryan sat down beside me without a word and patted my back heavily to make sure I wasn't gonna pass out. I'm still ashamed as I remember how badly I had behaved that day. Yet, this was not the end of the story.

Dear Jazz,

Being in love had turned me into a monster. Even though I could clearly see the truth of the situation, I just wasn't ready to let my Merlin go. A part me wanted to make him pay for the pain. I wanted to give him all my love and tear his out. This was the worst part of being a teen. You do things like an idiot. You believe in lies and deny the truth. You believe in the impossible and there's always a spark in you that never dies, that sheer part of will that still holds on to something. Mostly, the wrong wretched thing.

Had I been an escapist, I would've been blissful in my own corner of imagination. Had I been practical, I would've been content like Meera. Had I been idealistic, I would've been unconditionally devoted like Ketan. But no, I was a hopeful realist. No, worse. I was a hopeful realist, denying the reality. I was going insane.

Aryan was concerned about me more than anyone. It was because of his idea that Meera convinced mom and dad to take us for a trip to Dehradun and Haridwar. She dragged me around for 3 weeks, making me hike across arid, parched mountainsides on our way from Haridwar to Rishikesh and soak up the history of the place with her. I felt half-dead but I followed her anyway, like a thirsty kid following its nanny goat for solace. Meera took me diving into Ganga's perfection and slowly all the raw beauty of the place helped me find a little spark of faith in life. Gradually I managed to climb back from the edge of abyss. The black pit of my loss became smaller and smaller and slowly I was able to step aside from it and detach from the pain. By the time we got back to Faizabad, I was resolved. I would never let this happen to me again.

Dear Jazz,

It had been months and he still hadn't spoken. Not that I cared anymore. Meanwhile, Meera took to fashion technology in NIFT and I took to photography, against a lotta Engineer-IIT-IP-lovers. We were rigid on following our heart. And dad was totally on our side, though mom didn't show much of an interest in fashion and photography.

Now you might be wondering how I ended up being a photographer. Well, I was given my 1st camera when I was 13 years old. It was a Kodak Duraflex 2 from the 60's which belonged to your great grand mom. I kept it with me all these years and it still took pictures. Although I grew up in digital age, she insisted on teaching me how to use film cameras and develop pictures. She was primarily self-taught. All my role model forever.

I had to rent an apartment near Hazratganj in Lucknow, unable to survive the college hostel. Meera had no problems being a hostel late at NIFT in Bareilly. My best friend was doing BioTech in Vellore and my boyfriend was doing BTech at BHU. Life seemed all fancy you know.

Despite going to college to improve my skills, I've never been the one to follow the crowd. And I've never known whether it's good or bad. And that's why, in Ketan's opinion, I'm always better at it. I shoot from heart as well as head. It was like poetry to me. A lot of people would temme that when I'd set up a shot, even for a professional shoot, it's instinctive yet meticulously orchestrated.

I've always had passion for details in life you know. I'd notice small things that people would not even acknowledge: the texture of lips, a wisp of loose hair, the featherness of eyelashes, the dilations of pupils, the angle of an eyebrow arch, the roundness of a cheek or the slenderness of an ankle. I'd find these evocative. Often I'd create a frame with my fingers and choose a spot on Ketan's body (when he'd come to see me during hols) leaning close and examining the exact pattern of his skin until he'd prise my fingers off him and tease me for my obsession.

Ketan would come to stay with me whenever possible for a few days (mind, in different bedrooms) and then go back home to Ayodhya. Of course, our parents didn't know about us spending time like this. They didn't know about our relationship at all. They'd freak out like anything like any other Indian parents. So, we kept it to ourselves.

I'd miss him when he'd leave but I'd always have Aryan to ring up and talk my mouth off every day. Other than that I'd made quite some friends there to hang out with. Especially, Anushka my shopping guru who knew where and how to buy stuff in cheap; Monica who always had a lotta guys around to call a boyfriend every other week; Rudra the cool cat-talk of the town-party rocker. I had all hot messes to call friends you know;)

Dear Jazz,

Back in my apartment, I remember dressing up for one of Rudra's just- for- the-heck- of–it parties. His dad was a businessman cum divorcee, which meant that him being outta lucknow was a party night for his son. Not really a son. Um…very few people knew that he was gay.

I had Anushka and Monica for the ride it was quite a warm month of August for me to pull on black silk shorts, a small white sleeveless blouse tucked inside. I lengthened the tail of my eyeliner, did my hair to a high bun and chose black pumps over my usual flats to get a modern 60's look. I've always loved that look.

By the time we arrived at Rudra's party, it was in full swing. "Sameera!" he cried when he saw me, his eyes flashing from too much alcohol already. "you're gonna be the next Kareena Kapur! Where did you get that outfit? You look vintage!" we shared similar interests when it came to vintage. "It IS vintage!" I had to cry over Ishq Ki Maa Ki playing in the background. He hooked his arm through mine and brought me into the sitting room.

I balanced my glass of red wine in one hand and a cigarette in the other. I know, I know, this is not how you know me but if there's anything new my friends had ever taught me, it was this. And believe me it isn't so wrong sometimes. I didn't smoke but sometimes enjoyed the luxury of a cigarette with a drink. And Rudra's sitting room was thick with smoke already. I was disappointed to see that he had invited some of the dope crowd. But then, it was Rudra's party. EVERYBODY and ANYBODY is invited. I've never understood the attraction that most of my friends had for grass. I'd find smoking it ok, yet I'd never feel it's need to get outta my body, if that's what they're doing it for in the 1st place. Drugs in general didn't interest me, since my dreams were often psychedelic enough. I've never judged people if they wanted to take drugs but if everyone's smoking dope, I'd find that the party becomes a bit boring too early on and conversation is certainly limited.

I walked through the crowd as the song switched from Abhi Toh Party Shuru Hui Hai to Hamare Raja Ji Din Mein Na Bole Ki Raatiya Mein Chunari Khole. I pushed my way through the lounging smokers; a few of them called out to me, offering me a spliff but I shook my head and looked for Rudra. Where the hell had he disappeared?

I pulled the sliding door out to his green open backyard. It was good to breathe in some oxygen after the smoky confines. There were neon lights all over the place. I snubbed off my cigarette, balancing my wine glass on an empty plant container. There the music wasn't nearly as loud and the crisp air felt like a cool balm on my skin. I hadn't realized how hot it was inside. I walked around hoping to find a place to sit. It took a second for me to realize that I, along with a few people here and there, were inside a large enclosure bounded by wooden rails radiating from either sides of Rudra's bungalow. There weren't any tables, instead, knots of people mostly sat on or leaned against the rails.

I looked around to find a place for myself when a cupid's arrow shot me right through the heart as I saw this gorgeous solitary guy leaning against the rails and staring up into the twilight sky, lost in thought. He had his sunglasses on, a leather jacket and I could tell, quite a confident swagger. Maybe the wine was working it's way up to my head as I completely forgot where I was.

I began to idly wonder if he studied at our college or if I'd seen him anywhere before. He looked very familiar but just didn't seem to go with the crowd. In fact, I thought he wasn't even our age.

I started towards an empty section of the railings, just a little away from the hot solitary thinker. I propped my elbows on the rough wooden rails and took in the surroundings popping in the rest of my wine. I loved this solitude, where I could think and be whatever I wanted in my mind. I'd compose poems this way. At a distance, there were 20-30 bikes, pickups and trails, surrounded by their owners. I could see the glowing tips of the cigarettes some of them were smoking and hear the occasional clink of bottles. I felt like letting my hair loose. I sighed, as it fell over my shoulder till my waist and suddenly I sensed someone's eyes on me.

I glanced to my side and saw that lonely eye-candy approaching me. I honed in on him, my body viscerally pulled in his direction. I was getting caught up in a love-at-1st-sight-in-movies kinda moment when he abruptly stopped, removed his glasses and fiddled with his phone. I took my chance to my eyes off him and pretend to be busy myself. I pulled out my phone to find 2 messages from Ketan, 5 from Aryan and…1 from the person I least expected.

Gud evng, lady. Long time, no speak.

My eyes widened and I thought I better head back. I quickly turned around and bumped right into a chest. I momentarily lost my balance but was held back in place by the shoulders.

"I'm sorry lady, I didn't mean to sneak up on you like that."

I looked up at the eye-candy's face and was frozen for a moment at the sudden recognition. I stared at an equally astonished face as my heart sank…deep down…

Dear Jazz,

The world spun around me as I took in the face of the one I never wanted to see. It was a slap right across my face.

"Sameera..hello?" he blinked.

"Good evening sir…" I automatically put on my I-don't-care look. But I couldn't help wondering how Rudra knew. ..My Merlin.

"I didn't know you were in Lucknow."

"Well…it's been a few months…"

"Months!" he grinned and leaned on the rails "Yet, never knew."

"You never asked." I looked at my feet, banishing the return of a long forgotten ache.

"Still, I thought you'd tell me."

"Didn't know you were interested" I made an innocent face knowingly and went back to my initial position.

"But I am, always. I've so many good memories of you." He smiled and I ignored it as much as I could.

"Well, you didn't respond for a long time."

"Because it took a long time for you to turn 18" He looked at me with surrendered eyes.

I could feel the same old jolt returning into my veins. I'd better change the subject.

"So…how come you know Rudra?"

"Who? Oh, the boy who owns this place? Not really. His friends, my students, dragged me out here…" he looked around, longing to leave. He seemed pretty honest and it was Rudra's party. Literally, ANYBODY is invited.

"Then, aren't you supposed to be in there?"

"I was. But I couldn't stand the aura for long. Aren't you supposed to be with your friends?"

"Hmm…they're all having a great time. I just came out for some air. Where are those students of yours?"

"Still in there. Probably drinking and ogling your friends." He crossed his arms and looked at me. "So, Ms. Kulkarni, what do you do?"

"Photography." I finally smiled.

And like that we passed our time outside talking about life, career, politics, climate and all those boring stuff that people somehow find interesting. I was silently struggling all the time to keep my suppressed feelings suppressed and start a new kinda friendship with him. All though I was not able to shake out of the surprise of seeing him there, I tried not to present him with all the question marks on my face.

His life, as he said, hadn't changed much. I looked for any difference anyway. He wore white shirt and blue jeans. The full sleeves folded up to his elbows. His sun glasses hung on the 1st button of his shirt. His hair, just as before, was neatly combed backwards and his eyes were as deep-set and intoxicating as ever. I could sense that, like me, he too was looking for details as I noticed his eyes, although stealthily, but deliberately grazing all over my face. Na ji, not body.

He looked great but apart from that there was something wholesome and natural about his looks and the way he'd use is hands to explain things, as if to a child. And there I was, looking like a dolled-up buckle bunny, hoping to hook up.

Though interesting, there was a difference that I wasn't able to pin point. Maybe it was the unguarded, almost vulnerable look on his face as he looked at me. Whatever it was, there was no helping it.

Dear Jazz,

That night as I talked to my Merlin, a considerable part of my hatred washed away. I could finally see what he was thinking. He was waiting for me to turn 18 so that he could at least talk some sense into me. But as a 17 year old, it was like telling a 10 year old that Santa Clause doesn't exist. So he simply stopped talking to me so that I would helplessly shut up a bit and give myself some space to grow up.

After talking, what I remember is, walking inside the house with him, sharing a few drinks (though it seemed that I was the one drinking and he was just playing with his glass), introducing him to my friends, him introducing me to his students, one of them asking me for a dance and by the time I was done dancing, Merlin was nowhere to be seen. He had left without a word and I left with my girls, considerably snubbed.

I woke up the next morning with a severe headache. Stepping into the shower, I wondered if seeing Merlin at the party was a figment of my imagination. But the message on my phone was real. "gud evng lady, long time no speak." I loved the way he spoke. Always. You musta noticed that we both talk like vintage, like we're in a totally different era. I noticed there was another message.

Gud mrng Sameera, it ws a swt surprise meeting u last night. I c tht u hv grown in2 a beautiful young lady. It's intriguing but amazing tht u took photography , nyways, all d bst 4 future endeavours. God bless u. hv a gud day.

I held my breath. "All d bst..." I looked with dread. "God bless u..." what's that supposed to mean? He's going away again?! Anger flooded me. So, he was real the other night. He did temme that I was good. He did have a drink with me and now he's leaving again. He's teasing me! He's playing. Only, if I let him play this time. Never the less, I texted him good luck and a good day and went to tend my own work.

Remember, Jazz, nothing can hurt you, until or unless you allow it to. Nothing can make you feel guilty, unless you allow yourself to be guilty. If you wanna be happy, be.

Dear Jazz,

Months had passed and it was December when our semester hols began again. Ketan was coming for yet another stay, only this time he was to stay all weekend.

"How did your mom allow that?" I asked in awe.

"Why? You're not happy?"

"I am. But, how did this happen?"

"Well...my best friend had an accident and he needs me." He winked. "Sammy, I wanna take you somewhere, away from the city. I need to show you a place. That's why. Better start packing some stuff, we're leaving today, in the evening and we'll come back tomorrow."

"Today evening?"

"Yeah..."

I looked at him, puzzled. We have gone out like this before but never for so long. Nor had I ever had to pack a bag.

"Where are we going?" I was curious.

"Surprise, honey." He grinned.

I smiled but questioningly. I loved mysteries.

We left that evening at around 4 and I was getting more excited. "So temme something about the place…anything?" I pleaded and he drove a rented car.

"Well, I used to go there as a boy. Dad found the place. He was out this way trying to drum up business and he just kind of stumbled on it. It used to be a struggling summer camp but the new owners got it into their heads and now they can fill the rooms all year long. They made improvements to the place and the cabins. Mom totally fell in love with the place.

It took a little over 2 hours to reach the camp, the sky slowly filling with clouds that stretched to the blue peaked mountains dotted in the horizon. In time, the highway began to rise, the air thinning and turning crisp and we eventually stopped at a grocery store to pick up supplies where I wandered around taking pictures of everything. Everything we bought went into the backseat.

Ketan exited the main highway after leaving a town, following a road that curved steadily into a mountain itself. I can't believe, I still remember it all. It dropped off steeply on my side, the tops of the trees visible through the window. Fortunately, there was very little traffic, but whenever a car passed Ketan had to grip the wheel with both hands as the trailer wheels skirted the very edge of the asphalt. I wondered all the time if I was doing the right thing by coming out so far without knowing my own whereabouts and informing nobody but Aryan on the phone, just because I trusted Ketan. I was used to watching Savdhaan India. I couldn't help pinching thoughts.

When we reached the camp, I saw 12 cabins (too long and big to be cabins) spreading out in a semi-circle from a general store, which also doubled as the office. Behind the store was a pond, sparkling with the kinda crystal blue water found only in the mountains.

After checking in, Ketan unloaded the things we bought while I wandered off towards the ravine with my camera. I took in the view of the valley, more than a thousand feet and when Ketan finished up, he joined me too. Our vision wandering from one mountaintop to the next.

"I've never seen something like this before…" I murmured, awestruck, as we stood together. "It's breathtakingly beautiful."

"I was thinking about the same thing" he said. But I felt his eyes on me.

Dear Jazz,

I stayed in a daze only to put a few things in the fridge and notice the small bedroom, kitchen, drawing room and a clawfoot tub in the bathroom that we had for ourselves. My initial impression was one of fraying but pleasant hominess, a perfectly cozy overnight getaway, while Ketan was busy unpacking our bags. I couldn't understand how he dared to throw away his shirt and jacket on the floor in December.

"I think I'm in the mood for a bath before we eat." I said, eyeing him.

"Mind if I hop in first?"

"If you promise not to use all the hot water."

"I'll be fast. Trust me."

Leaving the bathroom to Ketan, I went to the kitchen and reached for a pack of Frootie in the fridge which I was crazy enough to warm up above the gas stove before drinking and thinking. As fun as college had been, I sometimes couldn't help thinking that my life had been on hold for the last few months. Swirling the Frootie in my hand as if like a glass of wine, I felt like a kid playing grown-up, like that stupid childhood game 'ghar-ghar'.

Unlike me Ketan seemed more like an adult. He seemed to understand everything: life, people, relationships, brains, career. Whatever we had between us was based in the real world not in the fantasy bubble of college life. Ketan was as real as anyone I'd ever met.

I heard the water shut off with a thump in the pipes, carrying the Frootie, I took a tour of the kitchen. Small, functional, inexpensive. Though the countertop had been peeling and rusty rings stained the sink, it smelled of Lyzol and bleach. The floor had been recently swept and the surfaces were dustfree.

I heard the water come on again and when the bathroom door squeaked open, Ketan stepped out looking clean and fresh in jeans and a blue jersey. He was barefoot and it looked as though he had raked his fingers through his wet hair rather than using a comb.

"It's all yours." He said. "I've already got the water running for you."

"Thank you." I gave his a kiss. "I'll probably be 30-40 mins."

I undressed slowly and slipped into the water in the tub, feeling luxurious despite the modest surroundings. The bathroom had a small separate shower stall where Ketan had hung his used towel on the rod. The fact that he had been naked in there a few minute before made something in my lower belly flutter. I tried to imagine what Ketan would be doing in the kitchen. I wondered if he was thinking about me soaked in the tub, maybe even picturing what I looked without clothes and again I felt a flutter in my belly.

When the water began to cool, I climbed outta the tub and towelled off. I threw on a pair of jeans, a form-fitting blouse and dried my hair. I touched more mascara and eye shadow than usual, wiping the old mirror to clear away the steam.

When I stepped out, I saw Ketan standing in the kitchen, his back to me as he stirred something on the stove. On the counter next to him, lay a packet of Kurkure and the Frootie I had left. I watched as he reached for it, taking a long pull.

He hadn't heard me leave the bathroom and for a while I simply watched him in silence, admiring the fit of his jeans and his smooth, unhurried actions as he cooked. Quitely, I bent down down at the end of the table to light the candles that I found in a drawer and turned off the light in the drawing room. The room darkened, becoming more intimate, the candle flames flickering.

Ketan noticed the change in light and glanced over his shoulder. I rememeber the look on his face as he saw me in my favorite pair of jeans and the blouse he'd bought me on Valentine's Day.

Whatever happened that night, we decided we'd better get back home the next morning, for we woke up on the couch, tangled in a sheet, half naked.

Dear Jazz,

As always, Aryan called after Ketan and I got back home I held up with his tantrums to know each and everything in detail. What could I have told him? I simply said that we spent a night at a quite place to get a break from the city noise and pollution.

"That's it?" he didn't even try to hide his disappointment. "No make-outs?"

"Naaaahhhh..." I repeated for the 8th time.

"Abbey (bleep) you missed your chance!"

"Seriously, stop asking. Or I'll hang up."

"O c'mon, it's so bound to happen. I know something happened! TELL ME!"

I hung up.

So, I spent the week with Ketan by simply going out for movies, restaurants, driving, shopping. Nothing sexy. We specially took care of it. Infact, Ketan was way more careful.

Pretty awkward though. He wouldn't come too close at all. When it started becoming too awkward, I had to ask.

"Sam, do you remember what happened that night?"

"Yeah, we got all hot and horny. So what? We didn't go too far."

"Yeah…we stopped." He paused. "Do you remember why we stopped?"

"Because…we fell asleep?"

"No. I mean, yeah, yes we did, but when exactly? What was the last thing?"

I thought as I answered. "We were going all overboard…so I gasped out your name. You got the point and you stopped."

He looked at me seriously. Almost angry.

"What? I just said your name. What's the big deal?"

"Think again." He commanded.

I thought. I tried to remember it all again. We sunk on the couch, me on him. My forehead resting on his. His fingers stroking through my hair. His lips making patterns on my neck. Tracing it's way up and kissing my lips. What began so softly, started to go a little wilder. His hands went inside my unbuttoned blouse, his bare chest rubbed against mine, his kisses became more and more vigorous and when his hand slowly slipped into my jeans, I gasped out his name.

He still wasn't convinced. I was missing something. I repeated the whole thing again and again in my head until the name finally touched my tongue again. THE name. I looked up at

Ketan, blood pulsing through my ears. I said a name. But it… wasn't his name. I looked almost horrified as the realization dawned. I had said…Vikram.

Dear jazz,

I vented all to Aryan, as always, after Ketan had left the next morning. I've never been able to admit this but, honestly, I couldn't see the point in being the same anymore. The part of me that I had been trying to keep suppressed was clearly way outta my control. Who the hell was I still kidding? I am who I am after all. And Merlin was an unforgettable and irreplaceable part of me. Why try to fool myself anymore?

Jazz, life is no game but neither is it a matter of life or death. Rather, it's more like a desperate D-, always getting hard for no reason. You too, will face some serious predicaments in life where the alternatives may seem equally good and bad. But that doesn't mean that you cannot be choosy. Take a bold step and don't ever regret it. Because whatever it is, it's something you really wanted to do and it had made you smile. I'm telling you, because I was in one such situation myself.

I loved Ketan, but I loved Merlin too. There's no mistaking it. Really, I was tired of running away from my own self. Jazz, when you love something, you let it go. If it comes back, it's yours. So, I decided to go jogging the next morning and look around. I didn't know where he lived. But a part of me was hoping that I'd find him again. If I do, he's mine. I'll make him mine.

I skipped down the stairs and stepped out of the outer gate in glee, the next day. I felt like a child released from her studies. The usually notorious city now seemed to be gleaming. How different Lucknow is when the sun is shining and so are you. It becomes a metaphor- a fragile ring of joy that can sometimes surround the bereaved. I thought about what I'd gone through in the past as I jogged through a quiet street that lead to a park at a distance. In the silence, I remembered how I was broken at the realization of my loss. How I'd felt when I knew that my dream was nothing but a dead end. How my eyes shone when I completed the 3rd diary writing about Merlin. I remembered the last line on the last page.

I love him, always…

But my grief was like the sun that day. This essentially melancholy street emblazoned with a sudden silvery burst of light. Such love I had for him.

I jogged as far as my tight legs allowed along the street and through the trickling traffic. I passed a hospital, just before the park, its marble façade so blindingly white in sunshine that I had to close my eyes. When I opened my eyes, I froze at place.

Right outside the park, I saw Merlin. I noticed him walking towards me and I wasn't sure if he noticed me as well. For a moment I thought about running back to the hospital to hide from him, just when I watched him bending down and stroking a black cat, which rubbed itself against his legs. I couldn't help thinking how I'd love to be that cat, especially when I saw him lift the cat's chin and feed it a biscuit.

He straightened up and walked towards me again. I was unable to move, forwards or backwards. Somehow I managed a step forward, yet he made no sign that he'd seen me. And suddenly I felt overwhelmed with shyness. Usually, I didn't have a problem looking or even ogling at men. I was adept at giving them the eye. Yet, that day I felt like a bashful young girl again. The girl I was at school. As he passed by me, I gave a quick sideway glance. Still, he was looking straight ahead, but I think I saw him smile.

I walked along feeling disappointed, yet as I got to the far corner of the park, I turned around one last time and was surprised to see that he'd done the same. Our eyes locked and I could feel the heat rising from my chest to my neck. I strived to remain calm and collected. The hell with Aryan telling me that Merlin's too old, to me he was the most gorgeous man I'd ever laid my eyes on. I felt a strange urge to flee and yet there was another part of me that couldn't step away. As if his gaze had me trapped.

I circled the park, perusing through the creepers of the fence, only to find him doing the same in the opposite direction. It was then that I grasped what he was doing.

Dear jazz,

He was playing stranger and was silently inviting me to his game. Staring up at the marble of the hospital, he walked in a circled towards me. I did the same, feeling like walking in an old movie. This time when we passed, he spoke.

"Have we not already met?"

I stopped and looked up, pretending that I'd just noticed him. Courage flooded me as I warmed in his admiring gaze.

"I thought writers had more imagination than to come up with a line like that." I said teasingly.

"I must say, you are quite wrong there." He looked at me with a wicked gleam in his eyes. "Most writers don't have any imagination at all. We have no need of it, since our fantasies happen to be true stories of life.”

“I’d love to hear some of those fantasies.” I suggested coyly.

“Certainly,” he complied, “But only if you tell me some of yours and how you saw that I’m a writer.”

“Well, the parker’s pen along with that leather covered diary in your pocket gave it away.”

“Ah! Ms. Clairvoyant.”

We walked back along the streets, chatting each other up. I looked at him in wonder. Not only because it all happened pretty unexpectedly but because I’d never been so wildly attracted to another person. I could never get used to the grace of his tall, lean body without an inch of fat and his easy way of moving. His hair I noticed was as black as mine. I couldn’t understand why Aryan thought that he looked old, for all I could see was a wonderful combination of masculine rogue and feline beauty. Even his hands were beautiful as they took hold of mine for a second as a car zoomed past.

“How very typical of me, not having asked your name.” he continued playing stranger.

I thought about the nick name he’d given me ages ago. “Cinderella.” I said, not looking at him.

“Very appropriate.” he grinned, obviously remembering the same. “I don’t think I’ve ever seen such a beauty in all land.”

“I’m sure that you say that to girls everywhere.” I replied as his eyes glinted mischievously. He didn’t deny my accusation and yet managed to charm me.

"Ah, but I cannot say that any girl has such beautiful hair as yours. So long and think, perfect for your delicious face."

As we walked through the streets, Lucknow itself seemed like another place. Our shoulders often brushed, sending a jolt through my body. All the emotions from the past came flooding in. My world began to tilt as if I was losing perspective.

"Can I invite you for a cup of coffee perhaps?"

"Sounds great. When?" I replied. I could sense the heat in my glance.

He looked down to his feet and then up to me."I'll find you Cinderella. Trust me."

Dear jazz,

Love is an awful game of hearts where you might either succeed in all glory or been drawn into the shadowy world full of pain. Especially for those youngsters, who may indulge in the darker side of desire.

I waited for a day, 2 days, 3 days…a week. Yet, no news from him. I began to spend as much time as I could in my apartment, against my friends, especially Rudra asking me to hangout. I'd sit in my tiny balcony and watch the traffic below. A whistle, a horn or a single vibration from my phone would send my heart spinning. But it's never him. Surely, my Merlin found teaching, meditating, reading on spirituality and drowning in loneliness way more enticing than me. I tried my best not to care, yet it was impossible. Every night as I'd fall asleep, I'd see his roguish face. I knew he was bad for me. I knew, for him I was just another girl craving him.

"He insulted you Sammy. He presumptuously told you that you are trapped." I listened to Aryan on the phone. "And he just made you remember what happened back then. How depressed you were, striking at the weakness. He's a predator Sammy, hunting vulnerable girls. Get him outta your head."

I repeated his words again and again in my head all day. Still, I hoped that maybe Merlin saw something in me that he'd looked for all his life, like had. I tried to distract myself with my girls, shopping, photography and parties but they weren't the same. I even considered hitting on strangers at Rudra's parties, yet when I'd set off looking for guys, I'd begin hunting for my Merlin's face among them. This would leave me even more frustrated than before, wandering home wearily at night and facing further bleeps from Aryan on the phone.

It was one such night when a thought suddenly struck me. Was this some kinda test? I didn't know for sure, he said he'd find me, but did he expect me to show him some faith 1st? I opened Facebook on my phone and texted him.

Making a lady long so much aint gentlemanly u kno.

Especially d 1 who cares.

His reply came instantly.

I'm no gentleman pretty. I shall remain indebtd 4 d care.

Hw r u evr gonna repay I wonder?

I think dere's anothr party dis weekend..

Dear jazz,

"Sam! You look vampish darling!" was Rudra's 1st comment as I joined him at his party that weekend. Monica looked at me up and down giving me an appreciable smile.

"Yeah, girl you do look good." Anushka joined. "I haven't seen you dress like that for ages."

I thought about it. I hadn't changed my dressing style consciously, but Anushka was right. I used to dress up a lot more before. I'd never been interested in looking like femme fatale or sex bomb. I didn't even have the figure for it and I found the idea of doing anything to modify certain parts repulsive. I'd seen skinny models with fake tits while photo shoots and it had only made me sad. They'd look like Barbies to me, like a joke, all outta proportion.

Sometimes, however, I liked to put on what my friends called a sexy costume to create another persona. And yes, that day I had someone important to meet too. So, I did feel the need to look more spikier than usual. But I didn't mean to go overboard.

"You are such a contradiction sometimes Sam..." Monica commented as I sidled next to her on the wooden table, not caring for a chair.

"So shy and so way out...all at the same time." Anushka was wagging her finger at me, her eyes sparkling playfully.

"I like to maintain some mystery." I replied, trying to keep my face straight and innocent when Monica leaned on to me, grabbing my hand.

"So where are you off tonight, all dressed up like that? Is there another party somewhere? Can I come?" I extricated my hand from hers.

"No, there's no party and you can't come 'cause it's a secret."

She huffed crossing her arms so that her ample chest spill all over them. "C'mon Sams, you can tell us. We're your friends." She whined, her eyes big and doleful, trying to hypnotize me with her false lashes and think kohl. I shook my head, looking out for Merlin.

"Oh c'mon Sammy, you are no fun at all!"

"Don't mind her," Anushka waved to me, "she's been in a bad mod since her Punjabi Munda went home." She turned to her. "aae Monica darling, don't you know our Sam by now? This is why she's such a good friend. Because unlike **some** people, she knows how to keep a secret."

"I didn't know I wasn't supposed to tell anyone about Rudra's man!" Monica defended herself and I wanted to burst out laughing. "How was I supposed to know that he wasn't outta the room yet? It was so obvious he wasn't straight."

"May be to you, since you are such a nymphomaniac." I chimed in.

"Who's a nymphomaniac? Rudra asked, returning with cans of Tuborg.

"Monica darling, of course!" Anushka exclaimed while Monica gave her a shove. "Hey, mind my drink!"

"Well, that's hardly news." Rudra said, settling next to me.

As usual, the party went all dope and boring and I went out with a glass of wine.

Dear jazz,

A piece of advice, avoid dangerous looking drunk strangers at parties if you are dressed all Beyonce.

"Do you have a lighter?" somebody asked as I stood outside.

What a corny line, I thought as I turned around. The guy in front of me was not at all familiar. "Sure" I took out a lighter from my purse and stepped forward. I was no smoker but I always carried a lighter. The stranger cupped his hands although there was no breeze. I hesitated a bit before looking at his eyes, pulling back. I noticed how long his lashes were.

"I like your outfit" he said, looking at me up and down.

Instinctively, I pulled down my tiny black skirt which had ridden up my thighs. I supposed I looked a little provocative. But then, everyone dresses up for Rudra's party.

"So, what are you into? Fashion or photography?" I ignored his comment.

He laughed shortly. Suddenly annoyed, I carried my wine glass and made my way around him, but he did all to block my way.

I tried to push my way past him but he didn't move quickly enough for me and I gave him a little shove, spilling the wine all over his shirt.

"I'm so sorry, but you didn't move outta my way." I said a bit embarrassed.

"I didn't realize you were in such a hurry to get away from me."

"I wasn't, I just…look do you wanna take it off? I can get some salt from the kitchen and we could try to remove the wine from your shirt." I gaped at my own stupidity for a moment.

"Sure." He smiled down at me, although it didn't seem friendly at all. He unbuttoned and peeled off his shirt, handing it to me. Not the least bothered that there were people around. He asked me soak it in water 1st, his eyes narrowed. I gladly accepted the excuse to get away from him.

Suddenly, he put his arm around my waist, pulling me with such a force, I almost fell down. He kissed me so violently that he bit my bottom lip and I could taste my blood. I struggled with all my strength uselessly until I saw someone grab his neck from behind and pull him away swiftly.

Dear jazz,

I staggered back and looked up. Relief washed over me as I saw Merlin right behind that scoundrel, his one hand holding the back of his neck and the other twisting his arm tightly to the back. I looked at Merlin, as he looked at me with those beautiful eyes and then glanced at his captive's face. I stood up and slapped him roundly across his face, but still he grinned at me, not the least unnerved. I saw a few people turn to watch us. Merlin still held him for me with ease, so that I could give a hard blow right on his nose. This time he started wriggling violently.

"Sameera, go inside!" I froze at my Merlin's sudden rage. He could probably see the shock on my face.

"Sameera," he asked calmly this time. "Why don't you go inside and join the ladies?"

Though I wanted to stay with him, my body seemed to obey his command. I ran back inside, past all the slouching smokers and up the stairs, into Rudra's bathroom. I locked the door and stood with my back against it, breathing heavily. I walked over to the mirror and saw the blood on my lip and my flushed cheeks. Only then I realize that I was still holding on to that bummers shirt. I threw it across the bathroom and splashed cold water at my face.

I wanted to stay all night in the bathroom but was forced to come out by a stoned friend of Rudra, banging on the door and begging me to let him in before he has an accident. Wearily I came back downstairs and surveyed the room. I didn't want another encounter with that dope. I went to the kitchen where both Anushka and Monica were ensconced, munching through a bowl of crisps.

"Did you see a tall guy with no shirt on?" I ask them. Anushka looked at me with big black eyes and I could tell that she was stoned, which also meant that she was mute too. Grass, however had the opposite effect on Monica.

"Sorry, did you say a guy with no shirt on? What did you do to him Sammy?" she laughed. "You're a naughty girl, ravishing some stranger like that."

"Yes, well, did you see him?"

"No no, wish I had. I'd certainly woulda liked some of that."

I sighed and went a few steps back on the stairs to have a good look at the crowd. This time I wasn't looking for the stranger but for Merlin. I sat down on the steps in despair. I'd missed my chance again. I was in no partying mood anymore. I stood up with a shock when I felt a warm hand on my shoulder.

Dear jazz,

I cannot explain the joy that filled me as I turned around to see my Merlin. He'd waited for me! He walked past me, a little ahead and then gave me a look, asking me to follow him silently through the crowd. That's when I noticed that more people had arrived and many were dancing in couples to Ishq Wala Love. As I followed Merlin, I watched his easy walk with his hands inside the pockets of his jeans. Before I even realized, my hand went up and held the sleeve of his blue shirt, folded up to his elbows. Un sure of what he'd think, I slowly let go of his sleeve. He stopped to look back at me and in one swift motion he pulled me closer to him. Instinctively, I grabbed his arm with both my hands, feeling a burst of energy. I thought we were going to the garden, but instead he took me through the front door.

We walked along the quiet road for a while, with no other light except from the moon. The music faded behind us. I didn't know why I was following him or where we were going. I knew how girls were lured by psychos and how things were done to them. That's how they showed it in Savdhaan India right? But somehow I still trusted this man. I looked at his face but couldn't make out his features in the darkness. I could only see the moonlight glinting in his eyes, giving him an angelic touch.

I wanted to ask about the stranger but I thought it was better to keep quiet. We walked on, our arms linked together, in a silence that was comfortable, till we finally hit a street light.

"So, lady," he said suddenly breaking the silence, "Coffee still interests you?"

I smiled. "Has always."

We spotted KFC and thank god there weren't many people because the only people there only made me feel more insecure about my dressing. We took the table at a corner and he took the seat diagonally opposite to me so that I was blocked from anybody's vision. I loved him for that.

We ordered coffee and Paneer Tikki and soon set into an easy conversation. None of us speaking of whatever happened an hour ago. We gave each other an abbreviated overview of our childhood till our coffee arrived. Apparently, he too had a crazy part of childhood that I kept reminding him off.

"Mrs. Ramamurthy, the heart throb of our school!" he said. I smiled watching his eyes roll.

"Did she know about your crush?"

"Huh." He waved his hand. "Never. I was just a little star in her galaxy of admirers."

"A galaxy, mm?"

"No doubt. Beauty and intelligence unparalleled. Even the girl students were equally crazy."

"Hope she wasn't married…" I hope she very definitely was married!

"We mentally murdered her husband over and over." He laughed.

Though it was an impossible little love of a child that was so many years, I was becoming sober again. The only reason behind my smile being the way he often looked at my lip where I had begun to feel a clot. Our conversation continued for more than an hour and soon my phone began to vibrate as I had expected, not that I cared. I didn't want anything to interrupt my time with Merlin but he noticed my phone too.

"We should probably be getting back" he said. "I don't want your friends to be thinking that I lured you out or anything." He winked.

I really wanted to spend more time but remember Jazz, no matter how much you want, do not let the guy know that you are all gaga on him. Or he might take you for granted. No matter how much you love anyone, you don't love them more than yourself.

"Yeah," I said "I don't want them to leave without me either." I avoided as much eye contact as I could.

And we walked back, retracing the same enticingly dark path, the music growing louder and louder as we approached. Soon we were standing at the door. Some of the crowd had left. Somehow it felt as if I had been gone for hours.

"Do you want me to come inside in case…"

"No, I'll just stick to my friends and…"

"And?"

"…and thanks for the coffee and earlier…with that guy.."

"Well, I was glad to help lady." I nodded and turned around. "Good night Sameera." I watched him start away.

It would've ended there- and later I would've wondered if I should've let it- instead I took a step forward and the words came out automatically.

"Sir, will we see each other again?"

He smiled, flashing his dimples. "Sure, another evening" he looked at me "And maybe you should wear something comfortable."

Dear jazz,

Now that's where it all began. We were back to being normal. Back to being how we used to be. Back to texting, calling, Facebooking, sharing pictures, laughing and maybe sometimes talk dirty, all for no reason. No, I didn't go begging around for his love. Maybe as a17 year old I thought it was romantic to be involved with a smart, intelligent, devil-may-care, handsome gentleman who could cook, sing, speak vintage and be a thorough sportsman capable of easily taking on scoundrels. But now I was smarter right? Right?!

Hi, u r free 2nyt?

Yeah, js hanging out wid my grlz

Hw long do u usually stay out?

Depends…usually 11

Cn u find a lil tym 4 me too?

Lemme c..k. I think I cn manage sum tym.

Hw abt 6 hrs?

Haha, gr8. Rmembr d restaurant v last met @?

B dere @ 8pm.

kk. wht do u want me 2 wear? Obviously

u didn't lyk my skirt..

told u, nythng comfy.

Hehe...k

"Comfy..." I thought, staring at my pajamas lying on the bed. "Commffyy…" I thought again, staring at the XL white tee in my cupboard. "Very very comfy…" I thought staring at my bunny-faced bathroom chappals. "But probably not something for a restaurant. Then as usual, I went vintage, pulling on a maroon knee-length skirt, ivory full sleeved blouse and black heels. I went neutral on the makeup. Just a bit of mascara and Vaseline on my lips. I let my hair loose, just the way he liked it and wore golden hoops. No sign of a sex bomb.

We met at the same restaurant, the same table, where we had our 1st dinner, Chinese. I kept wondering all the time what kinda relationship we shared. Through the dinner, we talked about people, ideas, news, movies and stuff but apart from that, the focus was on me.

"I don't really see what could bother you at the hostel…" he said.

"Nothing's wrong with the hostel except there's a lotta noise, disturbance and one is rarely left alone. You know, my solitude is precious to me. Too much of socializing drives me nuts and bolts."

"Is it like what people say? All pajamas and pillow fights?" he asked mischiviously.

"Of course not. More like, negligees and pillow fights." I teased.

"I'd like a place like that." He laughed.

"I bet. Who wouldn't?"

"So…what is it really like?" this time he asked genuinely.

"It's just a bunch of girls who live together and most of the time it's ok. Other times, not so much. It's a world with it's own set of rules and hierarchy, which is fine if you buy into those things and privacy is almost nil. It's not that it's too much to survive, it's just that…"

"You're different." He said, finishing for me.

When the dinner was done, he looked at his watch. "It's almost time. I wanted to take you to a place, if that's ok with you."

It was a little after 10. "Sure, but time for what?"

"For no-crowd. You'll see…it's ok if it's awkward. We can do it some other time."

"I said SURE."

"Ok, come with me."

He lead me to his car outside, a sleek, black, Verna, that I took my time gaping at before getting it. Inside, it smelled like mint, jasmine and leather. I hesitated when he started the engine but I didn't say anything. Everyone knew the stories, the guy comes around looking all pleasant and nice at 1st but as soon as he gets her alone…I mean that's how they show it in Savdhaan India right?

"Sir," I emphasized on the address. "I don't like surprises." I lied. I loved surprises.

"But I think you do like star-gazing. You told me once. About an year ago. Since, it's a little late now, there isn't gonna be anybody around. We're the people of silence aren't we, Sameera?"

I blinked. "We're gonna be star-gazing?!"

Dear jazz,

I remember regarding him. I didn't hear any warning bells, though I could imagine Aryan's skeptical face. But for some reason, again, I trusted him. It just didn't feel like he was coming onto me. I sensed that if I asked him to leave, he would without a word.

As he drove us past several buildings and junctions, I had a feel that we were leaving the heart of the city. Soon I could see trees on either side of the road. Suddenly we went off road, as he veered into a narrow path into the woods on my side. I could feel my heart pounding against my chest. To my surprise, we entered a large clearing where he pulled in the car. He stepped out and opened door for me before going to the back. I followed.

"You carry garden chairs in the trunk of your car?" I asked in disbelief.

"I carry a lotta stuff in the trunk of my car" He said, pulling them out and unfolding. Of course, he did. Didn't everyone? Aryan and I would have a field day with it.

I helped him set the chairs in front of the car. He asked me to sit and joined me in a minute after turning off the headlights.

"Comfy?" he asked.

"Getting there."

"Do you wanna trade chairs?"

"It's not that…it's sitting here, under the night sky and stars…with you." I laid my head back, looking up at the twinkling diamonds.

"Haven't you ever been out like this with anyone before?"

"Not a soul."

We sat there for a long time, simply staring up at the stars in silence. There was no other sound except from the critters,birds, rustling leaves in the wind and breathing. I smiled at the elegant slice of moon and then turned to look at Merlin.

"Sir, can I ask you something?"

"You don't need permission."

"You never told me anything about your-" love. The word got stuck in my throat. "-wife." Better. I saw his expression go blank for a second.

"How does it interest you, doll?"

"Because it's something I don't know or I might just be making a conversation."

"Which one is it?"

"I could tell you, but how much fun would that be? The world needs a little mystery."

He gave a short laugh and then became silent again. I didn't press him to answer. If he wanted to tell, he would. And I was lost in the moment anyway, admiring the crescent above and the stars that surrounded her. I felt like singing.

"Which phase of the moon do you like the most?" he asked. "the full moon, I suppose?"

I shook my head. "The crescent."

"Surprised but impressed…why is that?" I could feel his laser like gaze. I didn't wanna speak much. I was afraid that I might spill the words. I didn't wanna go begging for his compassion again.

"Because she describes me better than anything. I answered shortly. He waited for more.

"Sameera," I closed my eyes. My name just felt so good in his mouth. "I'd love to hear your thoughts."

What could I tell him jazz? That the crescent was incomplete, like mE? Or that it's sharp edge reminded me of an age old pain? Or that she's a beautiful being that seems to be fading away? Or that no matter how bright the crescent may be, she was surrounded by all the darkness in the world? Or that it resembled my soul looking for a fairytale in a world full of nightmares? What could I really tell him? I decided to remain silent.

"Ok, I understand…" he said.

"Do you?" I did all to suppress a sarcastic smile.

"Sort of. I guess, I shall call you Crescent now on." He gave me beautiful smile. His eyes twinkling, like the stars teasing me from above. I felt like singing him a poem…

Between the day and night, in twilight's sight

I wander around in the fading light.

No one can see me, no one knows,

The demon I travel with, the evil he shows.

There's no escape, no way to get out,

Because no one can hear me, not even one shout.

Trapped between two worlds, the light and the dark,

The never ending search for a bright glowing spark.

Will I ever escape his games of the mind,

The power he has on me, makes me so blind.

This demon resides in the depths of my soul,

But I will keep fighting until I become whole.

Dear jazz,

I couldn't sleep in the remaining hours of that night. Apparrantly, I had been thinking about that poem ALOUD. I absently sung it out and as if in a dream, I fell right on Merlin's chest. He didn't push me away, as I had expected, rather, he put his arms around me. I don't know how long we spent time like that, without a word, without a thought, without a move. I just listened to his heart beat to my own heart's delight.

We didn't speak even in the car, as he drove me back to my apartment. But our hands still held each other's all the time. We spoke only when it was time for me to get off.

"Crescent, thank you for the company and a great time. Good night and sweet dreams dear."

"Sir," I paused "I'm sorry for…that…I didn't mean to, you know, I got lost in the moment and…"

"Please crescent, I adore you."

When I got up the next morning, I was hyperventilating for no reason. I had to vent, seriously. But if I told Aryan, he'd probably kill me with words. I needed someone who is the least bothered. At least, not so close to Ketan.

"And then what?" Meera asked. "Don't tell me you slept with him."

"Of course not! It wasn't like that at all. We just talked."

"And?"

"…I kinda fell on him."

"And?"

"…he adores me…it was sweet."

"Adore…my dictionary says it means to love intensely."

I closed my eyes, butterflies fluttering all around. "Maybe."

"Oh." she paused in an attempt to stop herself from bleeping me.

"Don't hide your disappointment. Really."

"What?" she announced. "From the way you sound, I think you did wanna sleep with him."

"I barely know him!"

"That's not true. You've spent months texting, calling, partying, dining, whatever with him. Months! Sammy, that's a lotta talking…if it was me, I would've grabbed his hand and dragged him inside.

"Meera!"

"I'm just saying. He's seriously charming, I know. That's what caught you right?"

"He's a nice guy." I said, heading it off.

"Even better." She teased. "What a sexy old guy he is."

"Meeerraa!"

"I get it! You are different from me. And I respect that –really, I do. I'm just glad that you are done with Ketan."

"So, when am I meeting you new stud?"

"Hey, we didn't talk about getting together or anything ok?"

"How could you not talk about it?"

"Because we're different."

I hung up and opened Facebook after making sure that she understood that this has to be strictly between just the two of us. I went straight to Merlin. There was already a message from him.

Hey, wht's ur fav place?

U shud kno by now…

I kno a lot nd…say I'm confusd? *wink*

Haha..i'm not telling u then. U SHUD kno!

Hmm...lemme think..

K...

crescent?

Hm?

D pub lib. I'll c u @ 8pm.

Bingo! Tht's d place.

The public library was way more empty than usual. Not that many people were readers. Since it was about to be 9, rarely anyone passed by our table, where Merlin and I settled opposite to each other, having a serious discussion on a rising international issue: how can captain America be any less than Iron man? Anyway, the library closed at 9 and we strolled out.

"Your sister texted me on Facebook yesterday…know what?"

"Probably rubbish. She's the world's biggest flirt."

"Not really rubbish…she said 'I heard you've been getting along with my sis pretty well'."

"No surprise there, that's Meera all right. She says whatever she's thinking. No filter."

"But you obviously like her a lot."

"Yeah, she's kinda taken me under her wing whenever I've needed it…she thinks I'm naïve."

"Is she right?"

By the time I even began to answer, we'd reached a restaurant that I didn't even know existed. I had heard about Avista but had never visited.

Dear jazz,

Following Merlin, I entered the retro-type restaurant. Only then did I notice that we'd been holding hands all the time. While we waited for an approaching waiter, I looked around, praying that I wouldn't bump into anyone I know. It didn't seem like the kinda place regularly frequented by students- Dominos and McDonalds were more favoured by us everywhere- but this place wasn't completely unknown either. None the less, we requested a seat on the outdoor patio.

Heat lamps glowed in the corners of the patio, casting a blanket of warmth that took the chill off the evening chill. Only one other table was occupied by a couple finishing their meal and it was blissfully quiet. The view wasn't much but the soft yellow glow from the Japanese lantern overhead gave the place a romantic feel.

After we took our seats, he leaned towards me. We still held hands.

"You didn't answer my question. Is your right? Are you naïve crescent?"

"Yes in some ways."

Before 16 years of age, I'd never had a boyfriend. In high school, I was kind of a nerd and didn't have a lotta time to go to parties and things like that, how Meera did. Then came college. I mean, I wasn't a hermit and I knew what people did on weekends in college. I knew there were drugs and sex all the time, but it was mainly rumors and whispers I'd overhear. It's not like I saw any of it happening. During my 1st semester in the campus, I was shocked to see how open everything was. I'd hear girls talking about hooking up with guys they'd just met and I wasn't even totally sure what that really meant. Sometimes, I'm still not sure, because it seems like different people mean different things. To some it's just making out, to others it's sleeping with someone while to others it's something in between. I spent a big chunk of my freshman year trying to unscramble the code.

Merlin simply smiled as I went on.

And there were parties all the time and to a lotta people that meant booze, drugs or whatever. I admit that I drank too much a couple of times and ended up sick and passing out in the bathroom. I'm not proud of that but there are a couple of people I know who do that on every weekend or all weekend long. It's in the dorms, the off campus apartments, everywhere. But, I just wasn't into it and to a lotta people, including my sis, that makes me naïve. Added to that, I wasn't into that whole hook-up culture. Meera's never understood why anyone would want a real boyfriend in college. She keeps telling me that the last thing she wants is anything serious.

Merlin leaned back, arms crossed and looking quite amused. "I know a few guys who would be very interested in a girl like that."

"No, don't…'cause even though she says that, I'm not sure it's true. I think she wants something real, but she just doesn't know how to find a guy who feels the same way. In college, there aren't many guys like that. And why would there be? When girls just give it away for nothing? I mean, I understand why you'd sleep with someone if you love them, but if you barely know them? What's the point? It just cheapens it."

I fell silent, realizing that he was the 1st person I'd admitted this all too, which was strange. Wasn't it?

"Sounds kind of mature if you ask me." He said, leaning into the lamplight.

I raised the menu, a bit embarrassed by that. "What's the weirdest thing you've ever had for dinner?" I tried to change the subject.

"Ladies first."

"Aalu Paratha with Sambhar." I looked for any change in his expression. I was expecting at least a smile, which just wasn't coming. Rather, he seemed to consider it. "Your turn."

"Something like yours…fried Oreos."

I stared at him. "You are comparing Aalu Paratha and Sambhar with fried Oreos?"

"Have you ever tried a fried Oreo?"

"Sounds disgusting."

"Yeah well, until you haven't, you are not allowed to comment. They're good. Have too many and you'll probably have a heart attack. But every now and then there's nothing like it. Way better than fried pasteries."

"Fried pasteries?!"

"If you are trying to find a suggestion, like I said, I'd go with fried Oreos."

At first I didn't know how to formulate any response at all. Then with a serious tone: "I don't think anyone would eat such a thing."

"You'd be surprised." He said as our food arrived. "It could be the next big thing here."

Dear jazz,

As the evening rolled on, things turned out even more unexpected.

"Do you really understand sex and porn and all that?" he asked.

I stopped at my food and looked up with all exclamatory marks on my face.

"C'mon, I wanna know you, the child or the nymph."

"Isn't sex a way to procreate?"

"Please come out of classroom bio theories. It could be much more."

"Well, eroticm is an art that is so ridiculously shown and called porn."

"Please elaborate the art."

This was something I'd never discussed with anyone but Meera and she totally thought that I should be in some aashram or something.

"Sir, it mightn't sound very exciting. It'll rather be boring. I'm afraid you won't even stand my views."

"Despite high testosterones, I'm highly spiritual. I will stand. No option for you."

Kinky. I stared at him mischievously. He was challenging. Very very kinky.

"How does it interest you?"

"Oh, because it's something I don't know," he said, picking up my cues "or I might just be making a conversation."

"Which one is it?"

"The world needs a little mystery."

I sighed dramatically. "I thought writers had-"

"-more imagination than to come up with a line like that? My domain necessitates me to know everything dear."

"So you would've asked the same had I been a boy, huh?"

"Would that make me gay?"

I pulled my eyes away from him, heat rising up in irritation, "How I hate all these labeling. Gays, lesbians, heterosexual, homosexual, bisexual, asexual, sadist, masochist…narcist. I believe it's impossible to define a person's sexuality by a specific label. It's multifaceted, constantly changing and evolving."

"So, doesn't people of the same sex indulging in intercourse change anything?"

"Of course it does. Through sex we can purge ourselves and become new again. It's the most purest and innocent form of communication between two souls and at the same time, the most abusive form of interaction between two humans."

I finally looked up at him. Leaning back in his chair, he looked like a professor studying me, trying to figure me out.

"What interests you the most? Sex or Sadomasochism?" I couldn't help asking him. Instantly his eyes dropped, restraining a grin. He didn't say anything but I could see that the answer was sadomasochism. Moreover, he had DOMINATRIX written all over his face.

"Obviously, you're a dominatrix." I said feeling proud for no reason.

"I have poor vocabulary lady, rehem!" he laughed.

"A freak under the sheets. Better?"

"worse."

"A dominatrix dominates over his/her submissive in bed. It might even mean hurting. Most of them like to keep their submissives bound."

"I'm not sadist, my crescent." He looked at me wide-eyed. I loved the concern on his face. I was finally penetrating through his barriers.

"Actually, if the dominants among us didn't find an outlet for their natural instincts in a contained environment, if you know what I mean, most of us could be quite aggressive and abusive in our everyday lives" I paused to take a look at him. I couldn't help imagining my Merlin the angry, dominant, angry, ripping his shirt off, devouring me right here on the table…I blushed and dropped my eyes. "It's sorta like a therapy. And it's very brave and honest to admit to those instincts.

"And what about the submissives?" he asked, letting his guard down. I was winning. "Isn't that a destructive emotion, particularly for women?"

"Not really," I almost sang it out. "Many women wanna be submissives because in fact it appeals to our vanity. We are the centre of attention." I stated passionately. "And it's quite ego centric actually. When a dominator does things to us, it becomes purifying. Being a submissive is all about trust. A woman often taps into her hidden secret self."

He arched his eyebrows skeptically, yet decided to say nothing. Instead he asked "what attracts you the most crescent. To dominate or to be submissive?"

"Neither." I said, looking square in the face.

"C'mon doll, I've been honest with you, haven't i?"

"Actually…" I smiled naughtily. "I'd like to leave it for you to find out."

Dear jazz,

I realized that no matter how much I try to suppress the demon of that dead lovesick girl in me, I knew that I didn't love Merlin in simply here and now but that I'd never stop loving him ever. I don't know if I was ever fully conscious when I picked up my phone and texted him the very next day.

Gud mrng sir.

Gm crescent, didn't think u'd b up so early.

I'm always up early. Cn I ask u sumthng?

Y not?

R u free 2nyt?

Haha, whr does my lady wanna go?

Nywhr..If it's ok wid u.

Name d place.

Um…ever seen Twilight? It hs a 4th part calld

Breaking Dawn, it's up @ fun republic…

Hv read d book, hvnt seen d movie. K then,

2nyt, fun republic, breaking dawn. C u dere.

I couldn't believe what I'd done for a minute. That was the 1st time I had asked him out. As if like a date. It still beats me, where the guts had come from. I could already feel the initial Sameera returning. The dead was resurrecting.

Oh how I loved it when I saw Merlin's eyes almost bulge when he saw that evening at the theatre. Obviously, he hadn't expected me in a pleated grey skirt that ended just above my knees, showing off my perfectly stockinged legs, a scarlet tight fitting blouse and black pumps. But the highlight was my hairdo, 2 neatly pleated braids that reached till my waist. I looked so…me!

However, the fun didn't last for long. After the movie, we walked down the road discussing the characters of the movie and our beliefs in eternal love. Then it all went down in his one single question.

"Crescent, have you ever been in love?"

"I…" I looked down as we continued walking. Heat began to rise, and I let the fire build up in me till I could bear my words no more. "I fall in love with you every single day as if for the 1st time."I felt embarrassed by how tiny my voice became. He stopped abruptly and stared at me in bewilderment. No, it was more like…emotional. And suddenly, just like that day at the park, I wanted to flee again. Only this time I knew better. Jazz, I wasn't trying to escape from him, I was trying to escape from my own very self. All my emotions from the past began to fill me as I looked at his dark, emotional, empty face. The same heart ache returned, only this time like never before. So much that I couldn't hold back my tears. I was so ashamed of myself, how I let a man like him have such an intense effect on me. Could he not see the pain in my eyes? Could he not feel the love in my words? Could he not sense that I…I was…withering?

I could see the desire in his eyes that reflected in mine. He did have deep feelings for me but he just wasn't allowing himself to let it out. Let it all flow. His coldness made me so angry. I almost felt like hitting him hard on his face. How can somebody be so heartless?

"…but you're such a monster, you made me fall in love with you and then you just left without a word. You left me stranded, hanging on for you! What a monster you were!" I saw him flinch but I was so consumed in the passion of my rage. "I'm in love with you…" I wailed "and yet to you I'm yet another silly lovesick girl." I turned away from him, stumbling blindly in darkness, before he caught me in time.

"Crescent, Crescent." He held me with all his strength as I tried to run. I glanced around. There's nobody watching excepting the lone half moon in the sky. I could feel his breath on my lip, so tantalizingly close.

"Shush…" he gave me a smile and my heart slightly lightened.

"Love is hell, Crescent, it's surreal…"

"If loving you is hell then it's hell that I'll love."

"By the time you understand me all your love will evaporate."

"And condense again."

"Experience forever warns me that so called love is nothing ji but making love and moving on."

"Aren't you believing what you want to believe?"

"This is the natural outcome when longstanding beliefs are shattered eventually."

"And how did that happen?"

"It's been a long journey for me and you are just beginning yours …you will learn yourself."

"Why are you still with me then…"

"Your resilience and perhaps my reluctance to hurt your presumably true feelings…"

"If you care so much about my feelings then what keeps you from"

"Crescent, it is difficult for me to be involved with any girl who I can't marry."

"Ok…so this is it. You don't wanna be called a cradle snatcher, that's all?"

"I'm unable to understand the sense you want to convey. It applies to marital sex too and I'm not averse to getting intimate with the girl who I will marry irrespective of the age difference, it's after all only a number and ageless guys like me won't subscribe to it."

"I'm not after you for sex...to me, love isn't about going physical all the time."

"Then please explain what it is to you."

"I'd like to show it, it's better than explaining."

"I'm in a state of perpetual shock...what you saw in me that you have not seen in so many guys so far...I'm such a simple and mediocre guy with intense spiritual leaning..."

"I saw nothing yet everything. I don't have a reason and I hate admitting it. lemme put it the 'Drouet' way. I love you 'cause it's impossible for me not to. I love you without question, without calculation, without reason good or bad, faithfully, with all my heart and soul and every other faculty. Believe it, for it is true. If you cannot, then I being at your side, will make a drastic effort to force you to do so."

He grew silent, taken aback. For at least a whole minute, he didn't react at all.

"You are too good for me Crescent...and too shocking for me to react. I just know that I'm hard to handle Crescent, I'm a heap of emotional wreck who dreads company out of personal and psychological demons... and you are an angel..."

"Hard to handle. Not impossible."

"Huh! You are bad for me lady, and I know that I am even more dangerous for you. Yet…you are so hard to resist."

"Then why resist..."

"How can one love someone so much, you truly are an enigma." He said, brushing his lips against my forehead, where it burned my skin.

"I just can't let you …go."

He cupped my face with both his hands. "You win."

I stood amazed. "I win? Is that supposed to mean that-" he leaned in and kissed my lips so very tenderly, I could taste the salt of my tears on our lips. I caught a glimpse of the half moon through my tears, filling up to whole. He moved to my ear and whispered softly, "I lose, my little Crescent."

Dear jazz,

I cannot tell you the joy that filled me, my heart flying all around. I could go screaming and shouting down the street and dance about my Merlin. My heart beat was still racing and there were butterflies everywhere. But my body strangely remained calm as I walked holding my Merlin's hand to take metro home.

The carriage was half full and I tried to look like I was minding my own business, as Merlin let go of my hand and took a seat opposite to me. I stared at the ads on the other side of the train but not really looking at them. I tried to think about the movie we just saw and suddenly about all the possibilities to move through time. If I could go back, I'd be at the 60's of Bollywood. The jazz, the costumes, the expressions, the hedonism!

I cast my eyes around the carriage and imagined myself in a movie, travelling back in time. The other passengers became unfocused shadows, superfluous extras, as smoothed don my skirt, crossed my stockinged legs and clasped my hands n my lap. I was no more Sameera. I was Miss.Crescent, the acclaimed starlet of the black and white movies, on my way to a day's filming. I smiled to myself. This wasn't a metro in Lucknow but a street car in Mumbai in 1966.

As I was having this rather delicious fantasy, I found myself staring straight into the curious eyes of my Merlin. Within the haze of my dream, he stood in front of me, more real than any man I'd ever laid my eyes on. I couldn't help admiring his smartly dressed body, neatly groomed dark hair, he could've stepped right out of an old movie. He had the features of a screen model and he was looking right at me, blatantly.

It was impossible to look away. His eyes so deep, seemed to belong to a magician. It passed through my mind if I was being bewitched, 'cause I could sense my own eyes widening, lashes fluttering involuntarily, and my pupils dilating. The train stopped once, and a group of partying students of my own age, clearly engineers, got on, filling the space between me and my Merlin. Yet, our eyes found each other. In fact, the jostling bodies added to the eroticism of our optical connection. He could reach me only with his gaze. I tried to pull away from his hypnotic eyes but all I could manage was take in his face. Wavy salt and pepper hair, tanned skin, a square jaw with dark stubble. I could imagine the feel of that stubble on my naked skin and it made me shiver involuntarily. Merlin was still staring at me, and for a moment I thought if he was dangerous. What? I was used to watching Savdhaan India ok?

I tried to look down, up, away, anywhere but him. I thought about changing my seat but just when I was about to get up, he smiled. And that changed everything. The stranger game was on again.

His smile was engaging, open and teasing. I wished I'd brought my camera. The man was no danger. I tipped my head to one side and gave him a half smile, a question in my gaze. It was the most I could manage but it was enough. The group of students got off in between, leaving just the two of us in the carriage. Yet, neither of us spoke. It was if words would break the erotic spell between us

We both stood up at exactly the same time to get off. I walked towards the door, sensing he was standing right behind me. Just before the train stopped, he picked up my hand and swung me around to face him. His lips found mine in a perfect screen kiss. As the train stopped, I fell on his chest. He smelled of Bulgary, strong, true and enticing. The door slid open and we stepped out on the platform together in arms. No words passed between us. There was no need, for our eyes had already made an agreement on that bewitching train ride. We walked down the platform, up the escalarator, through the barriers and out into the windy night of March. The wind that was stormy at beginning, soon became torrential, only adding more to the eroticism of the moment. He put his arm around my shoulder in an effort to protect me and ran with me down the road, letting me lead him wherever I wanted to take him.

Once inside my apartment, it began to rain outside and we kissed again. Deeper this time. We clung together, feeling the shape of each other through our wet clothes. He took a breath and stepped back as I slowly undid the buttons of my blouse. I waited for him to speak but it was as if he knew what I wanted. No words. Nothing false. Just the blind truth of desire. Instead he arched one of his eye brows and spoke with his expression. He slipped out of his jacket. I noticed, despite his ardor, that he was careful to hang it on the back of a chair before unbuttoning his own shirt. I was pleased, the gentleman had high standards. White heat was rising between us like a summer haze as we watched each other undress, not yet touching, taunting each other.

We took our time, a bold, long, languorous dance of foreplay. We knew this might get us into trouble, yet the pure abandon of it, drove us on. I could really lose myself to him. I longed to touch him, smell him, feel him. A dream man from 60's alive and breathing in my own real life movie. He held my shoulder and pulled me closer to him, as I stepped forward. He was so much taller and his height only made me feel even more aroused.

He followed my lead, walking backwards through the debris of clothes. Once inside my bedroom, he took me up in his arms and carried me to the bed, the romance of it taking my breath away. He placed me carefully on the bed and knelt next to me, hovering above. He stroked my body with his fingertips and I found myself exhaling a deep guttural sound as if I'd never really exhaled properly. His silence was intoxicating, as if he knew that to speak would destroy the passion between us. I felt like a different woman all normality abandoned, just sheer delight and desire fueling me. I was the crescent becoming whole. What was making me behave in such a way? Was it the whole romantic notion of it as if we were living a scene in the film or was it my carnel need pulsing through me, the badness of what was urging me on? I didn't know, I didn't care.

His lips on mine, his taste so sweet, his touch so right, his scent so seducing, his arms cradling me. My heart was racing as our warmed bodies merged together. Deeper and deeper we went into each other, deaf to the rain outside. We rolled over and over. My skin, flesh, soul, singing to his touch. We were meant to be. As there had been some other power at play that night. Suddenly, I felt myself quivering, I was panting, crawling up the edge of my abandon, tipping over, so nearly, so nearly. His mouth met mine again, gently caressing the spot where I was bitten at Rudra's party and to my shock, I was coming, throbbing around him. I looked into eyes, sheer as onyx in his own sensations. He gasped as he joined me in a beautiful climax. Falling on top of me, so that we both were sinking into each other. How much this human being trusted me, how much I trusted him. How much we had fallen in love with each other.

I tremble when his darkness sweeps over me,

The strong allure of the unknown pulls me in his direction.

Seduced by the sweet scent of destruction,

I lose myself in his arms and give myself to the night.

Dear jazz,

I think back to the 1st few weeks of our affair. How exciting it all was, how different, how much fun we had.

The 2nd time we met, it started normally enough. He'd rung me up and asked me to meet him at Taj Hotel. I thought it a rather grand location but assumed that we'd have a drink and then move on to somewhere less lavish. However when I arrived at the hotel at the appointed time, there was no sign of Merlin. I wound my way through the armchairs and little tables, slightly daunted by the sheer luxury of the place. Yet, loving it's opulence. I sank into one of those chairs and ordered a drink. To my surprise, when the waiter returned, he handed me a rather bulky envelope. In front, in elaborate calligraphy was written Crescent.

I knew instantly that it was from Merlin, not because of the name but because he was the kinda man who wrote in fancy script. I tore open the envelope and a key fell out on my lap, along with a roll of black cloth and a small white card on which was written "put this on before you open the door." He musta meant the cloth. Part of me was incredibly annoyed. How presumptuous of him. This was only our 2nd proper date and he didn't believe in dining a lady? I thought of finishing my drink and marching out, leaving him stewing in his room. But, there was a part of me though, that had been aroused by this little game. How very naughty this was. Hadn't I known that the night would turn out this way? So what if it began the way I thought it would end? I was Crescent, an independent young woman and I could do exactly as I pleased.

So, I found myself, riding the elevator to the 3rd floor of the luxurious Taj. I'd always wanted to stay there but never thought that it would be that way. How could he afford it?

I stepped out into the corridor, my palms sticky as I clutched the key card. My pulse skipping randomely. What if he changed his changed his mind the moment he saw me? What if the magic had been for that one single night. Was this some sorta trap? I've seen it happen in Savdhaan India. Well, there's no turning back now. I surveyed the corridor, from left to right. Not a soul in sight. I slipped on the black blind fold and pushed the keycard into the lock. When I heard a click, I pushed open the door.

What an incredible night that was. In fact, Merlin did dine me but in silence. No chit-chat, with my blind fold on. I can still recall that 1st delicious fizz of cold champagne of in my mouth. He fed me and more shockingly, I let him. It was a meal I could never forget. It was Italian. He started with the sundried tomatoes, grilled aborigine and roasted peppers, succulent in virgin oil and rich with garlic. Next came spaghetti, laced with creamy pesto sauce. He fed me forkfuls of pasta and I imagined him looking at my lips, wondering if he was as turned on as I was.

"Now, Crescent, I have something else for you." I could make out the tease in his voice and it almost made me wanna giggle, an unusual sensation for me.

"Stand up please." He asked. He walked around and then I felt his fingers at the back of my dress. I'd worn a black dress with a zipper at the back, all the way down. "My, what a clever dress. Why do you always prefer black, Crescent?"

"I don't always wear black," I smiled crookedly "sometimes I wear nothing."

He whispered how stunning I looked as he unzipped my dress all the way to the hem, so it slipped off my body. He took my hand and guided me back to the chair. I started with a fright as he placed a plate on my lap. It was still hot on the bottom but not unpleasantly so. In fact, it started to spread more warmth, curling and melting me.

"Open your mouth please." He popped in a tiny spicy piece of I don't know what onto my tongue. I began to chew. It practically melted in my mouth. Food had never taste so good before.

I suddenly said that I wanted to see him. The game had gone long enough. He had fed me to the edge of my desire and now I wanted to see him. He let me, gently pulling off the blindfold. There was my Merlin, in the dimly lit room, looking as always, utterly irresistible. He pinned me with his gaze. "What about dessert?" he asked me levelly.

I arched an eyebrow giving him a rare smile. "Well I know what I can do with that. You are my dessert."

The night was full of sensations, the flavors, the textures and smells of different delicious food mixing with his scent. It was as if Merlin was able to unfurl layer after layer of the passion that lay within me. Just when I thought I had peaked, he took me even higher until we became two celestial bodies pulsing inside each other.

Dear jazz,

We'd become daytime friends and night time lovers. Vikram and Sameera in daylight, where as Merlin and Crescent under the night sky.

The pattern was set for our affair, we'd meet once, probably twice a week at hotels, galleries, parks, anywhere. We mostly met at different hotels in different parts of the city. We'd travel separately and meet at the appointed place. Somehow it made it even more exciting, illicit almost. After about a month, I began to take initiative. I'll never forget the time I sent him a text to meet me at another hotel.

I waited for him at the bar, ignoring the people staring at me. For some reason, most Indian men still find it extremely difficult to digest to see an Indian woman drinking freely. But so what? I was Crescent. The one that shines flamboyantly unaffected by the darkness around. Merlin came dashing into the bar, his hair laced with raindrops, his cheeks damp, his enthusiasm infectious. My heart lifted just to see him. He settled down next to me at the bar and smiled slyly.

"Can I buy you a drink?" he winked.

This is how we'd start, as if we were complete strangers. Meeting anonymously. Hitting on each other and flirting shamelessly.

After 2 glasses he asked me if I wanted to take my coat off. Certainly it was getting a little hot? I had had waited for the moment. I spun around on my stool, giving him a serious stare as I untied the belt of my coat and started unbuttoning. He watched in bemusement as I blew him a kiss, swung off my seat and sashayed out of the bar. Making heads isn't just an expression girl, you make it happen. Merlin followed me into the foyer and into the lift.

"What floor?" he asked, putting his hand over mine as I pushed the button and bringing it to his lips.

"4."

He stripped me off my coat in the lift, stunned at my audacity as he saw what I did or rather didn't have on.

"Why,Miss,Crescent, you are a shocking young woman." He kissed me deeply, before wrapping the coat around me again and I literally dragged him to our room. There we made intoxicating love at the very spot we landed as we fell through the door.

That's how it continued for almost an year. Gradually the spontaneity waned. But our love for each other remained just the same, deep and enticing. We'd mostly spend time stargazing at the same place in the woods in the safe embrace of each other. Sometimes he'd take me to beautiful places for photography. He never took me home and I never asked either. Certainly he was still haunted by the memories of his wife. I respected his love for her.

Over time, we had developed our own language in silence, sorta like a mutual connection that was extremely psychic. It wasn't a bit difficult. We both loved solitude. We both were highly intuitive introverts. When one was down, the other one would naturally gets a gut feeling that something's wrong without any specifics. Especially, after an incident at yet another hotel that left a deep impact on both of us. It affected me so much that I'd often get lost in my own world and would become really lonely. Nobody knew about it. I grew extremely quiet. I'd constantly need someone to comfort me and fortunately, most of the time, Merlin would be there for me. I'd often drive to where he took classes and silently watch him give lectures on personality development.

Then one day, I acquainted a shock that I'd almost forgotten about. I stood blankly at my door as Ketan smiled down at me and squeezed his way inside with a whole lotta luggage. The deal was that we'd stay together for a week, he'd take me on a tour to Varanasi to watch Ganga Aarti and stay there for another day at Radison's. He didn't answer me at all when I asked him from he got all the money stay at Radison's.

So, the next day I packed a bag and we took an evening train to Varanasi. We reached the next morning and the 1st thing was text Merlin about it. Of course, he knew about my relationship with Ketan, I couldn't lie to him. But we still stuck to each other. He didn't mind me with him, but just wanted to make sure that I was doing fine. The next few days went like a dream. We roamed the city in a rickshaw, Ketan showed me various places, took me for shopping, movies, the BHU campus and Ganga Aarti.

Jazz, if you are to ever visit Varanasi, I advise you, DO NOT TAKE ANY VEHICLE. Believe me, you'll reach anywhere faster on foot, for the place is nothing but a jungle of traffic and obnoxious humans crowding everywhere. By the time, Ketan and I reached back to our room, we were more dead with exhaustion than alive and we had an afternoon train, back to Lucknow the other day.

Dear jazz,

As always, I was up early the next morning, but turned out Ketan was already set for the day. When I hopped outta the bed, I found him wrapped in towel, emerging outta the bathroom.

"Morning Sam," he winked "I got the water running for you. Enjoy the bath princess."

Groggily, I grabbed my clothes and went in. I stood frozen for a moment inside. It was one of the most luxurious bathrooms I had ever seen. It was decorated in the style of hammam, with mosaic floors and candles flickering around. Ketan's phone was left on charge and I could hear Hungarian Sonata playing on it. How very nice of him. There was a large bath at the centre, filled with fragrant water bubbling with little jets. I could see the steam rising off it, looking quite so inviting.

I submerged my tired body under the aromatic water and stared open eyed at the ceiling of the hammam through the dusky dappled light. A memory came to me, unwanted and I imagined myself within it. I was in the same bath where that incident occurred at that hotel and Merlin was leaning over me, reaching for my hands and pulling me up so that I emerged spluttering and naked in his arms. He grabbed a towel and wrapped me in it. I felt swaddled and trapped, yet safe in his embrace. It had been 3-4 months ago, even less yet the memory came from faraway place in time. I could smell my own body that day. It's failing, it's loss.

"What happened?" he asked "why is there so much blood in the water? Are you hurt?"

I squeezed my eyes tight, pushing my head into his chest, my mouth a rigid line of non-communication.

"Speak to me" he cajoled me "speak Crescent, what happened?"

But I couldn't. It hurt too much. I wriggled to free myself from his embrace. I wanted to run away from him, into the bedroom and wait for him to go away. I didn't want him to look at me this way. I knew him. He'd take all the blame on his head and return to how he used to be. Drowning in guilt and isolation. Yet if I left, I knew he'd follow. I just stood there.

"Oh Crescent!" I heard his shocked whisper as he registered the reason for the blood. "Why didn't you tell me?"

So many reasons why. I didn't want the baby. I did want the baby. I didn't wanna love Merlin. I did love Merlin. I didn't want him to think that he was trapped with me. It was too humiliating a thought. I wanted him to love me. I wanted to face it on my own. And yet I couldn't. I wanted it all to go away…and now it had. And for some reason, I wished it were not so. I had been unable to answer him.

Back to the present, as I bathed in the cleansing waters of hammam pool, I looked down at my belly. In there…in there, was Merlin's child.

I placed my hands just below and on either sides of my belly and pressed it down gently. I wished our baby away. That's what I did. I felt a fluttering inside me and I panicked. Not the thought of having a child but at how I'd have confronted my family. How Merlin would accept it. I prayed for the baby to go. I asked it to leave. And it did. And I'll never forget the look on Merlin's face as he tried to comfort me. He could feel my pain. He knew how it terrified me.

Dear jazz,

Back in the premises of my own apartment, I felt better. Except that Aryan was shouting his head off on the phone, not failing to bleep me after every single accusation. According to him, I was cheating on Ketan to be with some uncle-ji. According to me, nothing's wrong as long as Ketan doesn't know and I'm not treating him any differently. Never had I ever offended him, never had I ever ignored him, never had I ever behaved coldly or been distant. I was still the same. I still loved him. I was still his Sameera, so what if I took out a little time to be my Merlin's Crescent? If I belonged to Ketan, I belonged to Merlin too. Yes, our age difference was a problem but how does it matter when it doesn't bother US?!

Never had Merlin ever pressed me to do something I didn't want to do, never had he been anything less than a perfect gentleman. The more time I spent with him, the more convinced I was that he was the sexiest guy I had ever met. Who else could do things, he could do? Who was smart, charming, selfless, reliant and tender? Who could take me to the most beautiful places around and stargazing. Give me a single genuine reason not to love him. And yet, the odds were against us.

The winter of 2013, Merlin rang me up to invite me to his place for a late dinner. It came as a surprise to me as it was the 1st time he was inviting me home. He gave me his address and the appointed time was sharp 12mins to 12am. It sounded like a game to me. I took a taxi to his place a bit early so that I don't get late, surely there had to be a reason behind the weird timing? It was 11:30 pm when I reached there and I decided to stay outside in the car for the remaining time. It was cold out there anyway and the taxi driver was rather chatty and entertaining. I gazed out of the window to take a good look at the house, it wasn't so big but it was definitely beautiful with a lovely fenceless garden, lawn, trees, roses…

I noticed there was no light on inside the house, it looked almost unoccupied but according to the address that Merlin had given me this was the house. When only one more minute was left, I paid the driver and stepped out shivering into the night.

I rang the door bell thrice and then knocked on the door when no one answered, only to find the door already open. I pushed the door a little more and peeked inside but it was just too dark. "Merlin..?" I heard myself as my voice echoed into the darkness. I pulled out my phone and rang him up. The next second, I heard the familiar ringtone of Merlin's phone, coming from somewhere inside the house. I pushed the door wide open and went in, searching for the switches. As soon as I switched the lights on, the door I had opened behind me banged shut to my shock.

That night, Jazz, my world fell apart. It was shattering. I don't even clearly remember how I escaped, early the next morning. I ran all the way back to my apartment, barefoot, not thinking at all about the bloody hand prints on my clothes or the fingerprints on my cheek as it stung even more in the unbearable morning chill. Despite the cold, I was sweating and panting. When I reached back safely into my apartment, the sky was just turning pinkish grey outside.

I spent at least an hour, sitting naked on the floor of my bathroom under the shower. I was at the verge of insanity. The memory of my Merlin…his blood-shot eyes…as he struggled to breathe…and I just watched as blood spluttered out of his mouth…gushing out of his chest… my hands clutching a dagger with his blood on it…I just watched…watched him in pain…watched him trying to drag himself towards me… I remember, the compassion in his gaze as he looked at me even in that devastating state and though his voice couldn't carry his words to me, he mouthed, "I adore you so much Cres…don't worry about anything…" andmy body collapsed.

I don't know for how long I cried under the shower, biting my wrist and pulling my hair in an attempt to control myself from screaming out loud…my whole body felt like burning. I could've done anything to stop it…but I couldn't. I was a sinner, I reeked of sin and I couldn't wash it off me. My Merlin, my only one…was dead. No, murdered.

That evening I sat the same way again when I was done borrowing a few things from Rudra, under the shower. Just more composed and relaxed, after calling Aryan but speaking nothing. Allowing myself to get lost, as the feeling began to get me: the dead weight of my legs from sleeping pills, the dizziness from the alcohol, the soft throbbing of my pulse as blood pumped outta my wrists…that's it. That's what I had been waiting for, that's the quiet comfort. My vision darkened as a strange tall figure broke in through the bathroom door and was trying to shake me, but I didn't care. I blacked out on the floor, lost, giving myself up to the beauty of dying…giving myself up to a faraway velvety voice whispering how adorable I was.

Gloomy day and wretched night,

This crestfallen heart has no knowledge of light.

No morphine kisses to numb the pain,

These poisoned tears I cannot restrain.

No cure to stop the burning itches,

No gentle touch to heal these stitches.

This desolate place is where I'll stay,

My hermitage till my last day.

"Maa…" Jasleen came into the room rubbing her eyes. Meera was too busy turning her sister's bed upside down, tearing up the pillows, looking for any more letters. Jasleen was shocked to see her mother like this. She looked almost mad with anger just before she saw the terrified little girl. Without a single word, she picked her up and went into the hall to look for her bag as Jasleen struggled out of her mom's grip. As soon as Meera found her hand bag and the car keys, she almost dragged the girl out of the house, almost manic.

She was completely out of her senses as she drove to the hospital like crazy. But she wanted to know the truth. She wanted to know what happened. How could her sister have such a mad affair? Was Sameera not as naïve as she thought, after all? Could she really kill someone? But why would she do this to someone she loves more than her own life? Or was it her at all who did it? Or was she being played? What happened in that house? Who the hell broke in when she was committing suicide? Look at her guts trying to make such a stupid suicide attempt all poetic and cool in a letter to a 6 year old…

There was just one way to find out. Crescent.